BLACK STALLION

The Island Stallion

The red stallion stood on the island cliff, silhouetted against the moonlit walls like a giant statue. When Steve Duncan saw him, he knew this was his horse.

His quest after the great stallion led Steve into a fascinating lost world—a world untouched since the days of the Spanish *conquistadores*. With Steve, the reader enters this dangerous world and meets Flame, the wild horse of his dreams.

The author of the popular Black Stallion series has written another exciting and moving horse story for young readers.

The
Island Stallion

by WALTER FARLEY

Illustrated by KEITH WARD

Random House, New York

DEDICATED TO
ALL BOYS AND GIRLS WHO LOVE
HORSES BUT NEVER HAVE HAD
ONE OF THEIR OWN.

Contents

The Island Stallion

1

Island of Lost Horses

━━━━━━━

Azul island. Latitude 14° 3′ North. Longitude 56° 28′ West.

The freighter *Horn*, nine days out of New York City, was a mile from Azul Island, and running parallel to it. The freighter's only passenger, Steve Duncan, stood beside the captain at the bow of the ship. Steve wore only a pair of swimming trunks, and his tanned, lithe body was wet with the spray that whipped from the prow of the *Horn* as she dipped to meet each oncoming wave. Steve had been waiting many hours for his first sight of Azul Island.

The captain passed his binoculars to Steve, saying, "We can't get any closer, Steve. Dangerous reefs there. I've never been this close before."

Through the glasses, Steve could see the long white line of churning waters foaming across the reef between the ship and the island. He watched the waters turn from white to black once they had crossed the reef. Surging forward, the waves gathered momentum and height, only to disappear within the mist which hung like a gray veil about the base of Azul Island. Then there would be a sudden, bursting whiteness again, momentarily blotting out the gray, as the waves smashed heavily against what Steve knew must be a formidable wall of stone.

But above the mist he could see more of Azul Island, for the rock, a yellowish gold in color, rose a thousand or more feet above the sea. It was this massive rock which held his gaze as the *Horn* ran the length of the island. It was unlike any of the other islands they had passed in the Caribbean Sea. Not only did it differ in color from the green mountain ranges Steve had seen, but there were no peaks or ravines or indentations of any kind over its smooth, bare surface. The top of Azul Island seemed to be rounded off at one height, and Steve could only think of it as a huge stone that had been dropped into the sea. It was cold and barren, as though vegetation would have none of it.

The captain said, "Azul means blue in Spanish. I don't see where it gets its name. There's nothing but yellow rock."

"There's supposed to be a plain at one end of the island," Steve said.

"We're about opposite it now," the captain returned, "but the mist is blanketing it. That is, if you want to call it a plain. From the sea, it's always looked like a sandy spit. Oh, it's somewhat rolling and green in spots, but a sailor might as well be drowned in the sea as to be shipwrecked on it. Azul Island is one of the most forlorn places I've ever seen." The captain paused and turned to the boy. "How did you know about the plain? That is, if you don't mind my asking, Steve? Your interest in Azul Island has aroused my curiosity. I was surprised that you even knew of it, because the only map you'll ever find it on is our large-scale navigation map of this area. And it's nowhere near any of the airline routes. I just can't figure out . . ."

The boy's eyes were still turned shoreward as he said, "A very good friend of mine, Phil Pitcher, now lives on Antago. He wrote me about Azul Island a few weeks ago."

"Phil Pitcher," the captain repeated thoughtfully. "I believe I remember him, Steve. Sort of a small, thin man, wearing steel-rimmed glasses?"

"That's Pitch, all right." Steve smiled. "I think he did get down to Antago on the *Horn* at that."

"He sure did," the captain said, laughing. "If you don't go to Antago on my ship, you don't go at all. We're the only line that puts in at Antago; it's too far off the shipping lanes for any of the larger lines to bother with. Sure, I remember your Phil Pitcher. He spent most of his time reading during the trip, but every once in a while he'd come out of his shell and tell me about himself. It seems he was a little worried about having given up a job he'd had practically all his life to go to Antago. He wasn't quite sure at the time that he'd done the right thing."

"He's sure now," Steve said quietly. "From what he says in his letters, he's happier than he ever was at home. He wasn't very happy at home. Pitch lived next door to us for as long as I can remember, and he was pretty much a part of our family. We all knew he hated his job. He was a bookkeeper in the office of a big lumberyard, and the job kept him inside all the time. He didn't like that. I guess everyone had heard Pitch say at one time or another that he was going to quit and go to Antago to live with his stepbrother, Tom, who had a sugar plantation there. But no one believed him. Then a little over a year ago he did it. Quit just as he'd said he would, and went to Antago."

"Good man," the captain said, smiling.

"Yes," Steve said seriously, "we were so glad he finally did what he'd always wanted to do. But we've all missed him very much."

"He certainly didn't talk like a bookkeeper," the captain recollected. "You should have heard some of the tales he told me about the Conquistadores and the Spanish Conquest. They were enough to make your head spin."

"Pitch was always interested in the Conquistadores. That was another reason he preferred to come down

6

here rather than go anywhere else. He's a lot closer to them here."

"Then it's Pitch you're visiting on Antago," the captain said.

Steve nodded. "He's been asking Dad and me to get down to see him. Dad couldn't make it very well with his work and all, but he wanted me to go. I had planned to visit Pitch early next summer, instead of coming down now when I only have a few weeks before school opens again, but . . ." Steve stopped, his gaze shifting uneasily between the captain and the shoreline of Azul Island. He hadn't meant to divulge so much.

The captain was looking at him questioningly, waiting.

"I—I mean I just decided to come now," Steve said, without meeting the captain's eyes.

Smiling, the captain said, "But you'll have seventeen or eighteen days on Antago before we pick you up on the return trip. Maybe you'll find that long enough to be there."

"Sure," Steve said. "Maybe I will."

A few minutes later the captain left, and Steve stood alone at the rail as the *Horn* rounded the island and made its way south toward Antago, twenty miles away. He stayed at the bow until he could no longer see the yellow, dome-shaped top of Azul Island, then went below.

In his cabin, he took a worn and much handled newspaper clipping from the pocket of his suitcase. It was a picture taken on the plain of Azul Island, and Pitch had enclosed it in his last letter. It was because of this clipping, and only because of it, that he was visiting Pitch now instead of waiting until next summer. He couldn't have stayed at home, wondering. . . . He had to know.

Steve's dark, somber eyes studied the canyon in the picture. He noted again the high walls, tapering down to the sea; the rolling, barren land in front; and the cliff at the end of the canyon, hanging two hundred feet or more above the floor. And then his intent gaze became fixed upon the group of horses running down the canyon before the many men who followed. The head of a man wearing glasses was encircled in pencil, and alongside was the notation, "Me."

A flicker of a smile passed over Steve's face before he turned to the caption beneath the picture. He read it carefully, slowly, even though he could have recited it word for word:

"CARIBBEAN ROUNDUP!—Last week a group of men from Antago traveled the twenty miles to Azul Island to spend the day wrangling the wild horses that inhabit that island. The horses are believed to be descended from those which the Spanish Conquistadores brought to this hemisphere centuries ago. The Government of Antago

permits thirty horses to be removed from
Azul Island every five years. The agent in
charge of the procuring, breaking and sale
of these horses is Thomas J. Pitcher."
Carefully, Steve folded the newspaper clipping and
put it away.

It was four o'clock when the *Horn* dropped anchor
a quarter of a mile from Chestertown, the port of
Antago. Steve had finished packing his suitcase and
was in the captain's cabin, awaiting the attention of
the man from the Antago Immigration Department,
who was talking to the captain. Through the porthole,
Steve could see the red-roofed buildings on the shore
and the green countryside behind the town. He was
taking it all in when he heard the man from the
Immigration Department asking for his passport.
Steve gave it to him. The captain rose to his feet, bade
Steve good-bye and said he hoped he'd have a nice
vacation on Antago; then he excused himself and left.

After stamping Steve's passport, the man from the
Immigration Department returned it to him, saying,
"There's a Phil Pitcher waiting for you on the wharf.
If you're ready to go in now, you can come along
with me."

A few minutes later, Steve followed the man down
the ladder at the side of the *Horn*. Below, rising and
falling with the swells of the bay, was a large, deep
rowboat manned by six burly Negroes. The Immigra-

tion official stepped into the boat and, helpfully, took Steve's suitcase as the boy followed.

The men pushed away from the ship and began rowing toward town. For a few minutes, Steve looked back over the stern. Already the *Horn*'s cargo hoists were lifting heavy boxes from the hold to the barges that had pulled alongside the freighter. In a little while she would be on her way again, and Steve felt a temporary surge of regret that he was not going along.

But quickly he pushed the thought aside and turned his gaze shoreward. Here, he thought, is the beginning. This is what I actually asked for. It wasn't the *Horn* or a trip through the Caribbean that I wanted. It was Antago. No, rather, it was Azul Island. Well, I've seen it, part of it at any rate. No, I'm not discouraged by what I've seen. Somehow, I had expected it to be different from the others . . . forlorn . . . forsaken by all save the horses. It makes Azul Island all the more interesting. I'll have to arrange with Pitch to get there some way.

A fishing boat passed close by, its sails billowing with the wind. And ahead, Steve could see other boats moored closely to the sides of a canal.

They went up the canal, finally turning in toward a wharf, alongside which there was a large shed. Steve looked for Pitch. At first he did not recognize him, for his gaze passed over the small, thin man wearing knee-length pants and sun helmet. Then the man regained his attention by calling to Steve and sweeping off his helmet, waving it vigorously. When Steve saw the steel-rimmed glasses they were all that was necessary for him to identify Pitch at that distance. Waving back, he replied to Pitch's greetings and his frequent questions called across twenty feet of water. Yes, Steve yelled back, he'd had a good trip. Yes, everything was all right at home. It was good seeing him, too. Antago looked fine . . . just fine.

And all the while, Steve was thinking, he's the same Pitch, all right. The short pants threw me off at first. I'd never seen Pitch's knees before. Just as knobby as the rest of him. His skin has darkened a lot from the sun, but his face hasn't changed any. Mom always said that Pitch had the softest, roundest face she'd ever seen. Just take one look at Phil Pitcher, she'd say, and you know right off that he wouldn't do a bit of harm to anyone.

The rowboat pulled alongside the wharf and Pitch got hold of Steve's suitcase, sweeping it out of his hands. "You don't know how good it is to see you, Steve!" he said. "I've looked forward to having you or your father down here for a visit. Tell me about him, Steve. And your mother? How is she?"

As they walked to the shed, Steve told Pitch all the news he could think of. He opened his suitcase for the Customs authorities, then shut it again when they'd finished looking through it. One of the Customs' men took out a piece of chalk and scrawled his initials over Steve's bag.

"Now we can go," Pitch said, leading the way. "I have the car outside. We're twelve miles from town."

As they drove through the crowded streets, Pitch pointed out the local sights of interest—the bank, the market, theater, hotel—and then concluded by saying apologetically, "They're really not much. Although," he added more hopefully, "I do think you're going to like our house. My brother Tom's house, that is . . . it's located on a high cliff overlooking the sea. A beautiful view, Steve, very beautiful."

"I'm sure I'll like it," Steve assured him. He said it with enthusiasm, knowing very well that Pitch was afraid he'd be disappointed in his visit to Antago. It made him a little uncomfortable. So as they drove through the outskirts of town, he asked Pitch many questions about Antago and his life there.

And Pitch promptly reacted to Steve's interest in the island. He told him about Antago's sugar cane, among the finest grown in the world, he said. And his stepbrother, Tom, had the largest plantation on the island. He was Tom's bookkeeper. Yes, it was a much better job than working in the lumberyard office at home. It was very easy compared to that, he confided to Steve. Really, there wasn't much to do except at harvest time. And the weather on Antago was always nice. A little hot just now, perhaps. But he could always stand the heat better than the cold. He had disliked the winters at home very much.

Steve pointed to Pitch's shorts and said, smiling,

"Nor could you get by with an outfit like that at home."

"No," Pitch returned very seriously, "no, you couldn't at all. And it's a shame, for they're so comfortable. We'll have to get you a pair, Steve."

The countryside through which they were now driving was heavy with green fields of tall cane, but occasionally there would be open pasture land with lush grass upon which cattle, goats and horses were grazing. Steve had thought it best to wait a while before mentioning his desire to visit Azul Island, but the sight of the horses caused him to consider bringing up the subject at once. What's the sense of putting it off? he thought. I like Antago all right, but only as a place from which to get to Azul Island. I've only a little over two weeks, and I might as well find out now if Pitch knows how I can get there.

Pitch had been quiet for a while but now he turned to Steve. "Steve," he asked, "are you still interested in horses? I remember that as a youngster you sold me about ten subscriptions to a magazine I never wanted just because you were going to win a pony." Pitch's tone was hopeful again, as though he was still striving to find something of real interest to Steve.

"Yes," Steve replied, "very much so. I've ridden a lot during the past year."

·"Good," said Pitch. "I was hoping you would be." He paused a moment and Steve noticed an intentness in his pale, blue eyes that hadn't been there before.

"I'd like to tell you something," Pitch went on, "that's been of great interest to me of late." He paused again, and Steve waited impatiently for him to continue.

"Yes, Pitch," Steve had to say finally. "What is it?"

"Do you recall the picture I sent your father several weeks ago? The one of our rounding up the horses on Azul Island?"

Did he remember it! "Yes, Pitch, I do. That's why I . . ."

But Pitch interrupted with evident eagerness to tell his story. "It was the only time I'd been to Azul Island," he began. "Oh, I'd heard about it, of course; Tom spoke of it occasionally. And before I arrived here he had written me once or twice about wrangling horses on a small island not far from Antago. But," and Pitch smiled, "you know I'm pretty much of a greenhorn about things like that, and I never really understood any of it. That is, not until I went to Azul Island with Tom and the others."

Pitch paused and glanced at Steve. Then, as though pleased with the boy's obvious interest, he went on: "I remember that we all looked upon our visit to Azul Island as very much like a day's outing. And we spent the time there imagining ourselves as cowboys. I couldn't help thinking, as we ran after the horses, how strange we'd look to any people from our Western states. All of us, of course, were wearing our shorts and had on our sun helmets because the day was extremely hot. We had no trouble chasing the horses into the canyon, because the island is very narrow at that point; and twenty of us, walking about thirty yards apart, I would say, easily forced the horses into the canyon. Tom was in charge because he was the only one who knew anything about horses. The rest of us were plantation men, laborers, fishermen and the like with no experience whatsoever in this business of wrangling horses. However, as I've said, there was little to it, because Tom told us what to do, and it was he who selected thirty of the most likely-looking animals to take back with us to Antago."

Pitch stopped, thought a moment, then said in an apologetic tone, "I must tell you, Steve, that the horses are small, scrawny beasts and not very much to look at, really. But if you'd seen the desolateness of that small bit of the island, with the sparse grass and only the few meager, fresh-water holes, you'd wonder that they'd survived at all."

Pitch paused again before adding with renewed enthusiasm, "But they have, Steve! Their breed has survived for centuries on Azul Island!" His words came faster now. "It was on the way back from the island, with the animals crowded into the barge we towed behind our launch, that I first learned of it. I was sitting next to the photographer of our weekly newspaper, and I mentioned that I had been surprised to find so many horses on Azul Island. He mentioned, very casually, that these horses were believed to be

descended from the ones which the Spanish Conquistadores rode centuries ago! I tried to learn more,
but that was all he knew. His editor had told
him, he said. It was just an assignment to him. He
wasn't really interested. It shocked me, actually,
because I've always been so very much interested in
Spanish Colonial history that I suppose I assumed
everyone else would be. To think that here was a
breed of horse the Conquistadores rode, and which
had survived all these hundreds of years, and no one—
not even Tom, who knew of my interest—had
thought it important enough to tell me!

"I went to Tom immediately and asked him about
it," Pitch continued gravely. "I asked him if what I'd
learned from the photographer was actually true. He
laughed. I remember his laughing very well. Of
course, it was obvious to him that I was tremendously
interested and excited. Tom told me to sit down and
relax, because, he said, there wasn't a bit of truth to
the story. He'd heard it mentioned every so often for
the past fifteen years, but believed none of it. It made
a good human interest story for newspaper readers, he
said, and I remember he also intimated that the editor
of the local paper, an old friend of his, was capable of
making up such a story for the benefit of his readers."

"Then it's not true," Steve interrupted, obviously
disappointed, ". . . none of it. But Pitch, how did the
horses get there, then? And why does the Govern-

ment of Antago leave them on Azul Island when they could have much better pasture land here?"

"That's what I wondered, too, Steve," Pitch returned, "and that's exactly what I asked Tom. His first answer was, 'How do animals get anywhere? They were taken there, of course!' To me, his sallies were most confusing. I didn't know what he was driving at until I asked him why the Government of Antago allowed him, as agent in charge, to wrangle the horses only once every five years. And why did they limit the number of horses to be removed? Why did they insist that enough horses be left on Azul Island to maintain the progeny of this breed? Why, indeed! if the story wasn't true?

"He just laughed at me for a long time. Then he said in his most cynical way, which can be so very aggravating, that he believed it wasn't so much the Antago Government which was interested in these horses as it was the Antago Chamber of Commerce! And then he repeated that it made a good story, a story that could be placed in many foreign newspapers to publicize Antago, which was what the Chamber of Commerce wanted! He even intimated that he wouldn't be surprised to learn some day that the horses had been taken to Azul Island from Antago for the express purpose of creating such a story!

"But I didn't believe a word Tom told me," Pitch went on. "By that time I was very much interested in

17

the subject and was determined to see it through. I decided to learn all I could about the colonial history of Antago, and anything at all that was available on Azul Island. I wasn't able to learn much here, because the people seem so little interested in the past. It's only the present and future that hold their attention. They talk all the time about how much more they should get for their sugar and rum, and why Antago should be provided with an air service instead of having to rely upon the few boats that stop here. Problems like these are all they care about.

"So I got hold of some books from the States and learned that at one time Antago was used as a supply base by the Spaniards!" Pitch's eyes were bright as he went on excitedly, "From here, Steve, those infamous Conquistadores, men like Cortés, Pizarro and Balboa, may have selected their armies, their horses, guns and provisions, and set forth to plunder the Incas and the Aztecs of their gold!"

Pitch paused a moment, then continued in a calmer voice, "I also learned that in the year 1669, British and French pirates succeeded in sacking Antago and driving the Spaniards from the island."

"And Azul Island?" Steve asked. "Did you learn anything about it?"

"No," Pitch replied. "Nothing . . . absolutely nothing as to its history. The report mentioned only that it was an uninhabited island twenty miles north of Antago."

"Then in spite of what Tom said, you think that the horses now there could be descended from the horses of the Conquistadores?" Steve asked with keen interest.

"I do, Steve. I most certainly do," Pitch said slowly. "The Spaniards surely knew of Azul Island and it's very possible that they could have used it for something . . . or were even forced to go there when Antago was sacked by the British and French pirates. I'm terribly interested," he added quickly, "because here's an island that's been avoided for centuries, except for the few visits by Tom and the others who preceded him to obtain horses. And for all anyone knows it's possible that there's other evidence besides the horses that the Spaniards once inhabited the island. I want very much to look around, because it's obvious no one else has."

"Pitch," Steve said quickly, "I want to go with you to Azul Island."

"You mean what I've said about Azul Island interests you as well?"

"More than you know," Steve replied quickly. "When can we go, Pitch?"

"Why . . . I guess most any time," Pitch said thoughtfully. "I'd planned on going when your father wrote that you'd like to come here. Yes . . . we could go any time you say."

"Tomorrow, Pitch?"

"Tomorrow?" Pitch's blue eyes met Steve's.

"Why, I guess so. I'm pretty much of a greenhorn when it comes to a camping trip, but I guess I have most everything ready for it." He paused, a look of concern upon his face. "You're sure you want to go to Azul Island more than anything else, Steve? It's your vacation, you know, and I'd hate to have you go there solely on my account."

Steve smiled. "It's not . . . it's on my own account that I want to go."

A few minutes later the car turned down a long driveway, and Steve saw the large house at the end. But between them and the house, not far off the road, he saw a corral. A tawny-colored horse with a long unkempt mane was running about the ring. Steve heard Pitch say, "There's one of the horses from Azul Island."

2

Bull Whip and Bottle

––––––––

STANDING in the center of the corral was a giant of a man, heavy limbed and long armed. In one hand he held a bull whip, and in his other the lead rope that was attached to the bridle of the horse which was running about the ring. The animal rolled its eyes restlessly, but it never actually ceased watching the man who held him. The man, too, had eyes for nothing but the horse.

Pitch brought the car to a stop opposite the corral. He and Steve were but thirty feet away now, and two men sitting on the fence waved to Pitch. But the eyes of the man in the center of the ring remained on the horse.

Pitch said, "That's Tom." He said it matter-of-factly, as though leaving it to Steve to draw his own conclusions.

Tom! This man was Tom Pitcher? This towering

giant, who could make six of Pitch? It was hard to believe, for never, Steve thought, had he seen two men more unlike each other. And these two were brothers! Stepbrothers, he reminded himself. But even so, he'd expected some resemblance.

The sharp crack of the bull whip brought his attention back to the scene before him. Trotting faster about the corral, the terrified horse snorted continually, his eyes shifting from the man who turned slowly with him to the long leather whip that lay snakelike on the ground between them.

Steve's gaze swept over the horse. Instinctively he noted the large head with long, almost mulelike ears; the shaggy, unkempt mane matted with dirt, and the small, wiry body bleached with dust and hardened sweat. Steve watched him as he moved ever faster about the corral, fearful of the bull whip which sprang at him like a striking black snake whenever he slowed his gait.

It went on for a long while, the man and the horse turning together, the rhythmic beat of hoofs over well-packed dirt, the sharp crack of the whip whenever the beat faltered. The horse's body was wet with sweat, and white lather was heavy about the bridle straps and the corners of his mouth. But his eyes, now dulled with exhaustion, never left the man in the center of the ring.

Pitch said, "Tom's way of breaking an animal isn't a pretty sight. Shall we go?"

The horse bucketed, coming down
with rigid forelegs

Steve shook his head, but said nothing. He wondered how long the horse had been running about the corral before they arrived.

The tired animal stumbled. The long bull whip cracked and the hard leather end caught the horse on his haunches. Snorting, he regained his stride and ran still faster about the ring. And all the time the man pivoted with him, bull whip raised and ready.

Would Tom never stop? Steve asked himself. How long did this go on? The horse was beaten now! What more did Tom expect? What satisfaction was he getting out of this driving, driving, *driving?*

And still the beat of hoofs went on, echoing more often now to the sharp, staccato cracks of the bull whip.

Steve felt he could take no more of it. He turned and found Pitch watching him. Pitch nodded and his hand went to the car's ignition switch. But before he had reached it there came a sudden end to the sound of hoofs and whip. Deadening silence settled about the corral. Together, Steve and Pitch looked back at the scene they had just left.

Tom was approaching the horse, the lead rope sliding through his fingers. The horse stood there trembling, his eyes alive with hate. Tom grabbed the bridle, then signaled to one of the men sitting on the fence. The man jumped down and, picking up a blanket, walked over and put it upon the back of the horse. Then Tom and the horse were alone in the corral again.

Steve saw Tom move to one side of the horse, carrying the reins. The horse sidestepped uneasily, his eyes following the bull whip Tom held coiled in his hand. Then, faster than Steve thought it possible for a man of Tom's weight to move, he was on the horse's back. Steve believed the horse to be too tired to put up a fight, but he'd never seen a wild horse broken before.

The horse bucketed, coming down with rigid forelegs. Up and down, twisting and turning, he flung himself about the corral. And Tom, his long legs wrapped securely about the horse's girth, stayed with him, flaying the heavy handle of the bull whip hard against the heaving body.

Finally the horse stood still, and Steve thought him surely beaten now. What more was left for him to do? His body could take no more, his spirit had to be broken after all this. But again he was mistaken. For suddenly the horse went down and rolled quickly over upon his back. But Tom had moved still faster. As the horse's legs buckled, he slipped off, avoiding the body which had sought to pin him to the ground. And now he stood at the horse's head as the animal lay on the ground. If the horse had wanted to stay there he couldn't have, for Tom whipped him to his feet; then he sprang upon his back again, cutting the bleeding flesh with the hard, blunt end of the whip.

In spite of the beating he was taking, the horse kept throwing his large head back, attempting to knock Tom off. Again Tom signaled to the men sitting on the corral fence, and one of them moved across the ring carrying a bottle.

With a sudden movement Pitch turned on the ignition switch and started the car's motor. "I've seen this once before," he said quickly, "and you'll be better off if you don't."

But Pitch was too late. As Tom held the bottle in his hand Steve saw the horse throw his head back again. Tom raised the bottle, then brought it down heavily upon the horse's head. The bottle broke, the contents streaming down over the head and face of the horse. He stood there, dazed, his body trembling, swaying.

As Pitch put the car into gear, Steve saw the broken horse walking slowly about the corral under Tom's guidance. Steve closed his eyes and felt sick at his stomach.

That evening at dinner Steve spoke little, and most of the time his eyes were upon Tom, sitting at the head of the table. There were moments when Steve thought he had a good idea of how the horse must have felt that afternoon.

At last, conscious of having been staring, Steve shifted his gaze to the chair in which Tom sat. It was a large mahogany chair, heavier and stronger than Steve's or Pitch's. It had to be. Tom's giant frame was slumped in it like a bulging sack of grain. Now he was leaning heavily over the table as he talked, his giant hands dwarfing the plate of food set before him. His long fingers, blunt and square at the tips, curled even now although he held nothing in them. No knife or fork, no bull whip or bottle.

Suddenly Steve heard his name mentioned. Looking up at Tom's dark, low-jowled face, he found the black eyes upon him, the thin lips drawn slightly at the corners in what could have been a smile. Steve could see the small, square teeth . . . teeth which looked as hard and strong as the rest of this man.

". . . that bottle didn't hurt him none," Tom was telling him.

So he knew, Steve thought. He was the kind of man nothing could be kept from for very long.

Tom had turned to Pitch. "Isn't that right, Phil? You've seen me use the bottle before. It didn't hurt the horse one bit, did it?"

"That's what you tell me," Pitch said slowly. "I don't know much about these things, but . . ."

Steve's eyes were upon Pitch as his friend groped for words in reply to Tom's question. It was apparent that Pitch, too, was uncomfortable. Perhaps, thought Steve, even a little frightened . . . as he was.

Settling back in his big chair, Tom laughed heartily, drowning out whatever it was that Pitch had meant to say. Then he turned to Steve again. "The top of a horse's skull is as hard as a rock," he said, his face unsmiling once more. "You could break a hundred bottles over it without hurting the horse."

How did he know? thought Steve cynically. Had he ever been a horse? Had he ever been hit heavily over the head with a bottle?

Tom hadn't finished. "It's not the bottle, but the water in the bottle that does the trick," he said. And now his voice was slightly contemptuous of their silent criticism. "The horse thinks the water is his own blood as it streams down over his head and into his eyes. It scares him. It scares him so much that he never forgets it, and you won't ever find him throwing back his head again." Tom settled back in his chair once more, as though awaiting their reaction to his full explanation.

Pitch was busy cutting his meat. Steve looked down and toyed with the food before him.

Silence hung heavily about the room until, suddenly, it was shattered by Tom's explosive laughter. "You're both too soft," he said angrily. And then, to Steve, "Why, I wasn't any older than you when I used my first bottle on a horse's head. We toughened up pretty young in those days." He stopped, turned to Pitch. "Or did we?" he added, smiling. "Perhaps I'm mistaken. Perhaps it was pretty much up to the man himself." Once more he addressed himself to Steve.

"Phil left England to go to college in the States, while I joined up with the British Army and went to India. I got put in the cavalry, and that's where I learned the bottle trick. We used to get a lot of our horses from Australia in those days. They were ugly-looking animals called Walers. Uglier than the ones from Azul Island, and much bigger, too. They had a nasty way of throwing their heads back at you. The way we stopped them was with the bottle." Tom paused, smiling. "Yes," he added, "first the bull whip, running them until they're groggy, then finish up with the bottle. It never fails to break a horse . . . one who'll give you a decent fight."

Steve raised his eyes and studied Tom. Was that it? he asked himself. Was it the thrill of overpowering an animal in physical combat that Tom enjoyed so much? Tom was looking at him, nodding his large head. Nodding as though he had no trouble reading Steve's every thought.

"Yes," Tom said, still smiling. "It's a pity that there were so few horses with any spirit in this last group from Azul Island. There were only three of the whole lot of thirty that put up any sort of a scrap. They seem to have less spirit than they ever had. Now, fifteen years ago when I first went to the island it was different. There'd be about ten or more who'd give me a good workout."

Tom was silent, and Steve thought he had finished

until he suddenly said, "There's no other reason I want to bring in these horses from Azul. They don't make any money for me. Nobody will pay much for them. And then ten percent of whatever I do get has to go to the Government. It doesn't leave me with anything. Oh, I didn't mind when I could look forward to a little fun, but if the horses don't show more spirit next time, I'll let someone else go to Azul Island."

And now Pitch was talking. Steve heard him telling Tom about their proposed camping trip to Azul Island, the trip he'd planned on taking for several weeks. Yes, Pitch was saying, he was still very much interested in the island in spite of what Tom had told him. He still believed that Azul Island had played a part in the Spanish colonization of the New World. He wanted to look around. Yes, and fortunately Steve too was interested in Colonial history. He had asked to go. They planned to spend two weeks . . .

When Pitch mentioned their intended length of stay upon Azul Island, Tom laughed harder than before, and his chair creaked as though in resentment of the heavy pounds of flesh and bone that made up this man. Finally he sat forward again, his elbows on the table and his fingers digging into the sides of his scalp. "Two weeks," he said. "Phil, you should know better, even if the kid doesn't. What in God's name are you going to do for two weeks on a spit of ground that's nothing more than a windswept reef? You'll go crazy. You won't spend two days there, let alone two weeks," he concluded, bursting into laughter again.

"I plan to do quite a bit of digging," Pitch said. "And Steve seems very much interested."

Tom turned to Steve, his black eyes smiling but probing at the same time. "You're interested?" he asked. "Interested in what?"

Steve's reply came quickly, instinctively. "Archeology," he said. And he wondered why he'd said it and how he had remembered a word he'd never used outside of his ancient-history class at school.

He saw Tom's brow furrow. Then Pitch said, "You see?"

"No," Tom returned, sarcastically. "No, I don't see. Nor can I see you two spending two weeks in that God-forsaken spot!" Pushing back his chair, he rose to his feet, towering above them.

"We'll stay," Steve said quietly.

Tom looked at him. "You've never been to Azul, and you're so sure?" he asked contemptuously.

Steve nodded without speaking.

Tom walked around the table, his eyes still on the boy. Then he came to a stop and Steve saw the smile on the thin lips again. Tom said quickly, "Phil told me the other day that you wanted a horse more than anything else when you were a kid. Do you still want one?"

"Yes," Steve replied, slowly. "I do. Why?"

"Then take a look at those horses on Azul Island

and take your pick of any one of them. If you stay two weeks on the island, I'll give him to you!" Laughing, Tom left the room.

Pitch was talking to Steve now, telling him what they'd have to do that evening in preparation for their trip to Azul Island. But Steve wasn't listening. Instead, he was thinking of Tom's parting wager. Two weeks on the island, and he could have his pick of any of the horses there!

3

Unpleasant Awakening

―――――――――

THE following morning they left Antago as the sun rose out of the sea, and soon were well out of sight of land. Pitch sat behind the wheel of the motor launch, his round face tense as the boat pushed its sharp prow into the heavy sea. Occasionally Steve heard him say something about being a greenhorn when it came to navigation, and that he was much better getting around on land. But Steve had little doubt that Pitch would find Azul Island. Pitch's boat, too, although an old one, was in excellent condition and very seaworthy. She rolled slightly with the waves, making Steve feel a little uncomfortable in the region of his stomach, but he felt that he could stand anything now that he was actually on his way to Azul Island.

It had worked out nicely, he thought. Pitch's own

interest in the island and his desire to go there had made it easy for him.

The hours dragged on, and the sun beat mercilessly down upon the open boat. Steve was thankful for the sun helmet that Pitch had made him bring along. Turning to his friend, he saw that Pitch was facing straight ahead, but with half-closed eyes, as though he were deep in concentration. Steve looked back at their wake and at the small dory they were towing. Pitch had insisted upon their taking it along just in case something should go wrong with the launch's motor. And lying in the back of the launch were the two shoulder packs that he and Pitch had crammed with tinned food, cooking utensils and the tiny stove. Beside them lay the folded canvas tent, and next to that the pick and shovel.

Steve's eyes remained upon the last-named objects. He wondered if Pitch would mind very much when he confessed to him that he really wasn't interested in digging up the earth in search of relics the Spaniards might have left there. Tonight he planned to tell Pitch exactly why he had come, why he wanted to explore every foot of Azul Island. And he wondered what Pitch's reaction would be to his story.

Steve remembered very clearly his first impression of the barren, mountainous rock of Azul Island. From the ship, it had looked as though no living thing could climb those sheer walls of yellow stone. Yet surely there had to be a way leading to the interior of the island. Still, Steve thought with concern, whenever Pitch had spoken of the island he had mentioned only the rolling, sandy plain. And Tom too had called it "nothing but a spit of ground . . . a windswept reef."

"Pitch," Steve said, "I was wondering about the rest of Azul Island. I mean other than the plain and canyon you've mentioned. How do you get into the interior of the island?"

"You don't," Pitch replied. "It isn't possible." Then, looking at Steve in puzzlement, "I hope, Steve, that you didn't think it was."

Steve couldn't keep the disappointment out of his voice. "I did, Pitch. I didn't think Azul Island just consisted of the plain you've mentioned." Then he asked quickly, "But what about the rest of the island, Pitch? There's at least nine miles of it. I know because the ship passed it on the way to Antago."

"Then you must know what a natural fortress it is," Pitch replied quietly. "No one could possibly scale those smooth walls of stone, even if he wanted to." Then he added with an attempt at humor, "Which no one has, of course."

"But from the canyon? Is there no way up from the canyon?"

The serious tone of Steve's voice caused Pitch to shake his head sadly as he said, "No, Steve, I'm afraid not. The canyon comes to an end up against the most precipitous wall of rock you've ever seen. There's an overhanging cliff about three hundred feet above the canyon floor, but that too, of course, is inaccessible. You'll see for yourself in a little while now."

In a little while now. You'll see for yourself in a little while now.

Steve repeated Pitch's words over and over to himself as the motor launch swept across the sea. He said them when the horizon was nothing but sea and sky. He said them when the yellowish dome of Azul Island appeared, the sun turning it into a glowing spire of copper and gold.

There was no mist and, very shortly, he could see the waves crashing against the walled barriers, sending their white fingers climbing frantically, eagerly up the mountainous rock as though the waves, too, sought an entrance to Azul Island. And then, their force spent, they would retreat, falling back into the sea.

But toward the eastern end of the island, the walls began their gradual descent, finally merging with the sea and becoming a long stretch of sandy beach over which the waves, unstopped, rolled high onto the shore. At one point, a narrow wooden pier extended into the water. Pitch steered the motorboat toward it.

In a little while now. You'll see for yourself in a little while now.

Steve helped Pitch moor the boat to the pier. He put on his shoulder pack and carried the folded canvas tent under his arm; then he followed Pitch

36

down the pier and stepped onto the beach. Stretched before him, just over the sand dunes, was the rolling land, and to his left, less than a mile away where the walls began their ascent again, was the canyon.

They were nearing the canyon when Steve first saw the horses. There were eleven of them, small and lean and shaggy . . . a stallion, who stopped grazing to look at them, and five brood mares with five spindle-legged fillies standing close beside them. It was obvious that Tom had left the worst of the horses upon Azul Island, Steve thought. Certainly the Conquistadores couldn't have ridden puny animals like these in their long, arduous campaigns into the New World! He remembered the pictures of statues he had seen in his schoolbooks of men like Pizarro and Cortés sitting astride horses strong and powerful of limb, capable of standing the rigors of long marches through strange and hostile lands. Thoughtfully he watched the horses until the stallion led his frightened, straggling band down the canyon.

Pitch said, "It's truly remarkable, Steve, that this breed of horse has survived at all in this place."

Steve bent down, picking up a tuft of grass. He tasted it, tasted the ends. Not the lush green grass of Antago, he thought, but hardy grass that could sustain life because it absorbed every bit of moisture in the ground.

"Of course," Pitch was saying, "they must spend most of their time in the canyon, where they're

37

protected from the weather and sun. The grass, too, is more abundant in the canyon." Pausing, he looked around, then added, "We'll make camp there, Steve."

They were approaching it now. The walls, a few hundred yards on either side of them, were rising, shutting out the sea. A quarter of a mile away, the canyon came to an abrupt end against a sheer wall of stone, the lower part darkened by shadows made by the sides of the canyon, the upper part shining like a living, golden vision in the sun's rays.

They walked into the shadows of the canyon walls, and for a few minutes Steve was blinded by the sudden transition from glaring light to soft darkness. Then his eyes became accustomed to the shadows, and he saw the end of the canyon a short distance away. The horses were standing there, grouped together, their frightened eyes upon the two humans. But Steve's gaze did not linger on the horses. Instead he looked upward, to the cliff that hung three hundred feet or more above.

Pitch said, "Now you can understand, Steve, what I meant when I said that it was impossible to get to the interior of the island from here. These walls make it impossible even to get up to the cliff." He was beside Steve, his eyes too fixed on the flat over-hanging rock. "And there'd be nowhere to go from there, either. Just look at that sheer wall of stone behind it!"

Pitch walked away but Steve stood there, still

gazing up at the cliff. Pitch is right, he thought, there's no possible way to reach the cliff from the canyon floor.

Then Pitch's voice reached him. He was calling for the tent. He wanted to set up camp. It was getting late, he said. The sun would be going down shortly.

Steve went over to him and threw his pack against the side of the canyon wall where Pitch had decided to make camp. But as he worked alongside Pitch, his eyes would turn very often to the cliff.

The sun sank rapidly behind the mountainous rock of Azul Island, and soon the darkness of night had sped from the canyon floor to the rolling, sandy plain beyond. Steve and Pitch had finished setting up the tent and now sat before the Sterno stove, heating a pot of beans and frankfurters.

"We should have collected some driftwood before it got dark," Pitch said, moving closer to the small flame emerging from the can of Sterno. "The night air is cool out here. It would have been nice to have a wood fire." Pausing, he added dismally, "I'm such a greenhorn at this, I'm afraid." He turned to Steve, who was still looking up at the darkened wall at the end of the canyon and who seemed not to have heard. Pitch pushed a fork into the frankfurters. "They're done, I think. Let me have your plate, Steve. Your plate, please," Pitch repeated, more insistently.

Steve heard him then and handed over his tin plate. "Thanks, Pitch," he said. He ate in silence for a few minutes, then looked up to find Pitch watching him. Smiling, he moved closer to his friend and the small flame. "Sorry," he said, "I was thinking about something." Then he added quickly, as though to make up for his inattention, "We should have gathered some wood from the beach, Pitch. A good fire would have been nice tonight."

Pitch looked at him, nodding. "Yes," he said, "it would have been nice." Steve certainly must have been thinking about something . . . and very intently too, Pitch mused, not to have heard him mention the same thing just a few moments before. He wondered what it was that occupied Steve's mind.

They finished eating in silence, each alone with his thoughts. The short neigh of one of the horses echoed throughout the canyon. Pitch turned in the direction of the horses, then to Steve, whose whole attention seemed to be fixed on the small flame before them. Pitch said casually, "We should have a full moon tonight. It'll be coming up soon." The boy was still looking at the flame and Pitch couldn't tell whether he'd heard or not. "A full moon tonight, Steve," he repeated, louder this time.

Steve roused himself from his reverie. "That's right," he said slowly, "it will be full tonight, won't it?" Then he was silent for a while, and only his eyes betrayed his restlessness. Finally he asked hesitantly, "Pitch, have you ever had something happen to you that you could swear had happened before?" He paused, groping for the right words. "I mean something you couldn't have done, actually."

Pitch was confused. "I don't quite understand what you mean, Steve," he replied with concern. "Do you mean something I may have dreamed?"

"Perhaps," Steve said. "Perhaps you could call it a dream . . . only something much more real and vivid than a dream."

Pitch attempted a smile which failed utterly as he saw the intent look in Steve's eyes. "Sometimes," he said seriously, "I do something which I have an idea I dreamed about before. I suppose it's the association of things. It's never been really vivid, though, and I'm never quite sure I actually dreamed it."

"This is very different from that," Steve said slowly. "And it's all here . . . now. All this," and he looked out over the canyon floor.

The expression on Pitch's face became still more confused. "I don't understand, Steve," he said. "Perhaps you'd better start from the beginnning."

"The beginning," Steve began slowly, "was ten years ago when I had that operation for my abscessed ear. You must remember it." He paused while Pitch nodded in agreement. "Then you must remember too," Steve went on, "how badly I wanted a pony at that time. I couldn't understand why Dad couldn't buy me one, if he could get me a scooter and a tricycle. I had to have a pony, so I tried getting one by myself. I sold subscriptions to a magazine that offered a pony as a prize to the kid getting the most new subscribers." Steve paused again, smiling as he added, "Yes, you were one of my best customers, Pitch. But I still didn't win the pony. So I continued drawing pictures of ponies and horses, making myself more miserable and Dad and Mother miserable as well, because they couldn't afford to buy me a pony, much less stand the upkeep of one."

Steve's eyes met Pitch's. "I'm telling you all this, Pitch, because it has an important bearing on what happened during the operation." Steve gazed back at the fire again. "I remember that the doctor came to the house, and he found me in bed, shrieking for a pony. I saw him nod to Dad, and then Dad was telling me I could have a pony if I would only lie still. So I relaxed and thought how wonderful it was going to be to have my very own pony. It wasn't long before the doctor's nurse put something over my nose and mouth. It was the anesthetic, but I didn't know it. I breathed in the sweet, sickly odor, and I was still thinking of my pony when the fiery pinwheels started. I followed them round and round as they sped faster and faster. Soon they were going so fast that they no longer made a circle, but were one ball of fire. It came at me hard, bursting in my face.

"It was then that I first saw Flame. I didn't name him Flame. The name just came with this horse, for his body was the red of fire. He was standing on the cliff . . ." Steve stopped and glanced behind him, ". . . that cliff," he added huskily. "Below, too, was the canyon and the rolling land beyond. All this . . ." His hand pointed to the canyon and then fell to his side. "It was all very vivid, Pitch . . . so vivid that when the operation was over I found that I had a red horse named Flame. Ponies no longer interested me, and when Dad brought up the subject of the promised pony, telling me that he hoped I'd understand why he couldn't keep his word, I told him that it was all right, that I didn't want a pony anyway. Then for months and months, every time I ran from the house, trotting to the park, I was riding a giant red stallion, the most wonderful horse in the world!

"I grew up," Steve went on, "and put Flame to one side along with my tricycle and scooter. But I never actually forgot him, Pitch," he insisted. "I never forgot Flame, nor the canyon and cliff. Then a few weeks ago your letter came . . . your letter with the picture of a place I'd thought an imaginary one for so many years!" Steve's voice had risen and there was eagerness in it now as he turned toward Pitch. "How could I have seen this canyon ten years ago, Pitch? How could I, when I'd never heard of Azul Island until a few weeks ago when your letter came? That's what brought me here, Pitch," he confessed.

Pitch was silent for a long while after Steve had finished. And when he finally spoke it was with reluctance, as though what he had to say would have been better left unsaid. "But Steve, you did know of Azul Island."

The boy's eyes were bright as he said quickly, "I didn't, Pitch! I couldn't have known of Azul Island when I was only seven years old!"

"You knew of it when you were only five," Pitch replied slowly. "Not by name, of course. Nor did I."

"You! What did YOU have to do with it?"

Pitch was uncomfortable. "I was the one who told you about it," he said, his eyes avoiding Steve's. "I was visiting your father one day when you came into the room to show him a drawing of a pony you'd made; then you showed it to me. You sat on my lap and I told you a story about horses. It was a story based on one of Tom's first letters to me from Antago. He had written of going to an island not far from Antago to wrangle the wild horses that were there. He described everything in great detail, including, of course, the canyon and cliff. I passed this all on to you, making it as vivid and real as I possibly could. And you and I pretended that we were with Tom, going down the canyon, watching the horses run ahead of us. We had a lot of fun making believe . . ." Pitch stopped and his eyes met the boy's. "I'm sorry, Steve, real sorry."

"Don't be silly, Pitch," Steve said, angry with

himself. "I guess I knew all the time there had to be an explanation for it all. But," he went on, smiling a little, "I guess I was trying to convince myself that something very unusual had taken place, that for some strange reason I was being told of an island where I should go." His voice dropped. "I suppose I even expected to find Flame here. It's my imagination, Pitch. At least Dad would call it that," he concluded bitterly.

Pitch was quiet for a while, then he said, "But there's nothing wrong with having an imagination, Steve. Let it loose now, here on this island." His voice became eager, excited. "Azul Island has been uninhabited by people since the days when Spain ruled the world. Think of the relics, the historical treasures we may find hidden within this canyon. We'll look around tomorrow, Steve. We'll do some digging, you and I!"

"Yes," Steve said softly. "Sure, Pitch."

4

The Stallion on the Cliff

―――――――

T HAT night Steve lay awake for a long time, his head protruding from the tent so he could watch the moon as it flooded the canyon with its light.

Why think about it any longer? he asked himself. There's no sense to it any more. You have your explanation for it all. What more do you want? Flame? Sorry, but he's part of your little dream, too. You'll have to give him up along with the rest. No, of course you don't want to, he taunted himself. It was nice having Flame again. You felt much the same as you did when you were seven, when you first rode him through the park, didn't you? Pitch's picture of Azul Island brought everything back again. But Pitch's explanation tonight brought you back to reality as well. Now you know how silly you've been, coming to this island in search of an imaginary horse. Too bad you can't have him. Too bad there is no Flame. But there are other horses here. They're nothing like your imaginary Flame, but they're horses nevertheless. Tom said he'd give you one if you stayed two weeks. You've always wanted a horse of your own, so here's your chance. Tomorrow you can take a closer look at them. Tomorrow you can take your pick of them. Yes, and tomorrow Pitch wants to start digging. Pitch, the historian. Steve, the archeologist. You'd better go to sleep now. It's getting late, and the moon is well up . . .

Steve didn't know how long he'd slept when suddenly he found himself wide awake again. He must have slept for some time, he reasoned, for the moon was directly overhead. What had awakened him? It seemed to have been something loud and shrill, like a whistle. He must have been dreaming. Pitch was sleeping soundly beside him. The night was very still. Yes, it had been a dream. He'd better go back to sleep again.

He had just closed his eyes when he heard the loud snort of the stallion, followed by nervous neighs from the mares. Then there came the sound of restless hoofs against stones.

Steve opened his eyes, wondering why the horses were moving about. An animal? Perhaps. Maybe even the moon. He'd heard somewhere that a full moon could make horses restless. He turned over on his stomach, looking at the small band grouped near the

47

opposite wall of the canyon. The moonlight made everything very distinct and he could see that all the horses were on their feet, moving about nervously. The stallion was trying to keep them together. One of the mares neighed loudly and it was echoed by the whinnies of the others. Several tried to break away from the group, but the stallion cut them off. He tossed his head, snorting repeatedly. It was obvious to Steve that the stallion was keeping the mares from breaking away. He watched for a long time, his eyes never leaving them. Finally he saw the stallion turn his head away from the mares and raise it high, snorting loudly. The other horses too moved about more restlessly than before.

At that moment the canyon echoed to a high-pitched whistle. Shrill, loud and clear, it vibrated from wall to wall until it lost itself in the rolling plain beyond. The whistle was like nothing Steve had ever heard before, and his breath came short. Then he forced himself to turn his head upward. Slowly he raised it until he could see the cliff high overhead.

A horse stood there, silhouetted against the bare moonlit walls like a giant statue! His small head was raised in haughty defiance, and the only thing about him that moved was the long mane that swept back in the night breeze.

Steve had stopped breathing. He closed his eyes. It's not true, he thought. I'm dreaming. Nothing is

48

true. I'm still asleep. I heard nothing, saw nothing, actually. Pitch is asleep beside me. The horses are asleep. I heard nothing. And nothing is on the cliff. Nothing, nothing, nothing!

But he opened his eyes and looked again. The horse was still there. Steve could see the high crest upon the long neck, the giant body which seemed so much out of proportion to the small head.

"Oh, Pitch! Pitch!" Steve shouted, pounding the sleeping figure beside him. If this were all a dream would he feel his fist sinking into Pitch's back? Would Pitch sit up, as he did now, grabbing him, shaking him by the shoulders?

"Steve! What on earth is the matter? Stop it!"

Then it's not a dream, Steve thought. This much of it, anyway. "Look up on the cliff, Pitch. Tell me what you see. Quick!" His voice was tired, beaten.

He watched as Pitch turned his head toward the cliff. For a frightening few seconds Pitch's face disclosed nothing. Then his eyes widened, the corners of his mouth twitched nervously, and he said, "I see a horse . . . a horse on the cliff! Incredible!"

Steve closed his eyes. When he opened them again, he looked up at the cliff. The horse was gone, the cliff deserted. Pitch's gaze met his. "We're sure, Pitch?" Steve asked. "We actually saw a horse standing there?"

Nodding, Pitch replied in a voice so low Steve

49

could barely make out his words. "I saw a horse. I'm sure I saw a horse," he said, ". . . but I can't believe it."

Steve too found it difficult to believe what only a few hours ago he would have accepted so eagerly and without question. But that was before Pitch had explained to him why he had always known this canyon of Azul Island.

The two lay on their blankets through the long hours before dawn, each knowing the other was not asleep, each alone with his thoughts. And every so often, first one and then the other would raise his head and look up at the cliff, only to find that there was nothing there.

The sky was becoming a dull gray when Steve said, "Pitch."

"Yes, Steve."

"We're both very sure now?"

There was a moment's silence before Pitch replied. "Yes, very sure. We couldn't both have had the same illusion."

"No," Steve agreed, slowly. "We couldn't have. It was a horse, all right . . . a very beautiful horse." He didn't call him Flame. He didn't think of him as Flame. He didn't know whether this horse was the color of fire or not. He didn't care. This was no imaginary horse upon the cliff, but a giant stallion, very much alive. This was no dream, for Pitch too had seen him. This was reality. A horse had stood upon the cliff only a few hours ago.

Pitch said, "He was there. But how did he get there?" To Pitch, the horse on the cliff meant that there had to be more of Azul Island that was habitable than this canyon and the plain beyond. Otherwise, where could the horse have come from? It seemed impossible for the greater part of this island to consist of anything more than mountainous yellow rock, just as he'd told Steve. Yet he must be wrong, because living proof had stood upon the cliff.

They rose with the dawn and ate a hurried breakfast; then, without a word to each other, made for the end of the canyon. Arriving there, they looked up at the cliff, then cast their eyes over the sheer canyon walls. Very slowly they walked about the canyon, examining every foot of the walls in search of a possible way to the cliff from the canyon floor. Finally they were back from where they had started and Pitch said, "I'm certain now that he never reached the cliff from this canyon. It's impossible for a human to do it, much less a horse."

"Then he had to come from up there," Steve said slowly.

"But from where, Steve?" Pitch asked incredulously. "Look at that sheer wall behind the cliff!"

Steve said, "We can see it rising *above* the cliff, but actually we can't tell from down here what happens when it *meets* the cliff. There may be a cave or path or something. There *has* to be a way. He got there."

"Yes," Pitch agreed, "there has to be a way." Then he became excited. "Do you know what this means, Steve?"

"It means there has to be more to Azul Island than you thought," Steve returned.

"More than anyone thought," Pitch corrected hastily. "More than anyone has ever dreamed! Why, Steve, the presence of that horse up on the cliff has to mean that the Spaniards did inhabit this island at one time! How else did that horse get up there? Could Tom or anyone else now have the audacity to tell me that the Antago Chamber of Commerce was responsible for him, too? Not for one moment, Steve!"

Steve smiled at Pitch's last remark, but the intent look in his friend's eyes convinced him that Pitch had not intended to be humorous. "You're right, Pitch," Steve said seriously. "And what we have to do now is to find a way into the interior."

Pitch shook his head sadly. "I'd give five years of my life to do it, Steve," he said, "but I don't see how. I really don't. Certainly we can't get up from here."

"No," Steve agreed, "but there's the sea, Pitch," he added eagerly. "We can take the launch and look for a place where it might be possible to climb up."

"I doubt that we could even get close enough to look, Steve. The waves would crash us against those stone walls. You've seen them. You know."

"But we could try, Pitch," Steve insisted. "There's

52

no other way." He paused, then added slowly, "Unless you just want to stay here in the canyon."

"No," Pitch denied quickly, "I never could be content to stay here now! You're right, Steve. We must do everything we can to get into the interior. This is probably the most important thing that's ever happened to either of us. Come on, we'll get the boat and see what we can find."

A short while later they were in the launch and running alongside the island. The launch rolled on the giant swells that crashed heavily against the walled barrier of Azul Island.

They had gone a good distance when Pitch said, "I'm afraid I was right, Steve. We can't get close enough to the island without cracking up, much less try to find a possible way up the sides. It's no use."

But Steve's eyes were turned shoreward toward a bursting spray of white foam, where a wave had struck something just before reaching the walls of Azul Island. In the few seconds before the next long line of waves rolled shoreward, Steve saw a dark greenish rock that rose from the sea only twenty feet or less from the mountainous shore. "Pitch," he said, "I see something. Bring her in closer here."

Cautiously Pitch brought the launch around, his eyes never leaving the waters in front of the prow. "We really shouldn't, Steve," he said gravely. "There are far too many submerged rocks along here."

Momentarily Steve glanced into the clear waters

about them, and he too saw the black shadows of the rocks below, some rising higher than others and easily capable of putting a hole into the hull of the launch. He heard Pitch mumbling something about being a greenhorn at a time like this. But the launch kept its slow, steady course toward shore as Pitch skillfully avoided the rocks.

"Tell me what you see, Steve," Pitch said, without taking his eyes from the swirling waters.

They were but thirty or forty yards away from the large moss-covered rock, and coming in just to the right of it. Steve watched a giant swell descend upon the rock, and waited for the white, foaming waters to pour from its sides. Then he saw a long narrow rock behind the larger one. "Pitch!" he shouted. "There's another rock behind the big one that's just ahead of us. It goes right up to the wall!"

Another swell struck the large rock, and this time Steve watched the waters as they cascaded off its sides and swept past both rocks until they rolled up against the yellow walls of Azul Island. He noticed that the waters struck the walls with little force and then would roll seaward again until they were stopped by the incoming waters that swept around the big rock. The result was a small channel alongside the two rocks, of swirling but navigable waters.

"What is it, Steve?" Pitch asked impatiently, as he turned the launch away from the shore. "We can't get any closer. It's too dangerous."

"We could get in there by using the dory, Pitch," Steve told him excitedly. "The big rock stops the waves before they get to the wall. The waters flow around it and alongside the smaller rock behind until they strike the wall. But they don't have any force, Pitch. They just slap up against the wall and then roll back until they meet the next wave coming around the big rock. The result is that it's fairly smooth close by the smaller rock. We could get in there with the dory, Pitch. We could slide her in alongside the big rock just after a wave has struck, then pull her up onto the smaller rock, directly behind the big one, so we'd have her to get away on."

"It sounds too dangerous," Pitch said thoughtfully.

"But Pitch, what else can we do? And if we're careful it shouldn't be dangerous."

"I don't know, Steve," Pitch began, ". . . there may be an easier way further on. We'd better go all the way around the island first."

"Okay," Steve said dismally, "but I doubt that we'll find anything else. If there was an easier way of getting on to this part of the island it would have been discovered long ago."

"I don't think anyone has ever looked before," Pitch replied insistently. "We wouldn't have either if we hadn't seen the horse last night," he reminded Steve.

"Yes, I guess you're right," Steve agreed. But as

the launch pulled still farther away from shore, he continued looking back at the waves striking the dark, greenish rock.

They were well out of danger from submerged rocks when Pitch turned to Steve, saying, "We'll go around to the other side of the island now, and if we find no other way, we'll come back in the dory as you suggest, Steve."

As they rounded the tip of Azul Island, the wind whipped into their faces and the launch dipped deeply into a far heavier sea.

Steve said, "It's worse here, Pitch. We wouldn't have a chance of getting in. The wind is driving the waves too hard against the walls on this side."

Pitch nodded grimly as the launch was tossed heavily about on the rough sea. "You're right, Steve, we'd better go back."

"For the dory?" Steve asked quickly.

"For the dory," Pitch repeated solemnly.

5

The Search

─────────

Two hours later, after having taken the launch back to the pier, they returned in the dory to the large green rock they had seen earlier. They had broken camp, and now their shoulder packs, along with several coils of rope and Pitch's pick and shovel, lay at the bottom of the dory as the small boat lightly rode the high swells.

"Perhaps it was silly to bring all this gear along," Pitch said. He was sitting beside Steve, both pulling hard on their oars. "Even if we're able to reach shore, we may not find a way up the sides, you know."

"But if we do," Steve said, "we'll be glad to have everything with us. It's too long a row to go back for it."

The dory fell swiftly into a deep trough, then rose high with the next swell. Steve saw that they were nearing the large rock, and his face became set.

Pitch said warningly, "Careful now, Steve."

A moment later they stopped rowing, but their oars remained in the water, directing the course of the dory and holding her back from riding in on top of the swells. They were both tense, for they knew that if they went too far to the left they would be swept against the rock and too far to the right would mean being carried all the way in against the walls of Azul Island. There were only a few feet of swirling waters where they could bring in the dory safely.

A heavy swell slipped under them and crashed against the rock, its spray coming down on top of their heads. As the dory went down into the trough before the next swell, Steve said, "Now, Pitch!" Together they plunged their oars downward and pulled hard. The small boat leapt ahead, its prow parallel with the rock. The wave behind them struck the face of the rock and water poured in torrents about them. Steve's fingers clawed at the jagged stones as he pulled the dory forward, and Pitch struck his oar viciously into the water as though he were wielding a canoe paddle. The dory's prow pushed sluggishly into the strong current flowing back from the walls of Azul Island, and for a moment Steve thought they would be pushed back to the front of the rock again. Then the waters from the rock surged forward to meet those coming from the wall. Now there were turbulent waters beneath the dory, but neither a forward nor backward current.

They were just behind the larger rock, and Steve saw the small alcove where the smaller rock joined the larger one. While he steadied the dory, Pitch jumped out onto the rock and grabbed the boat. "Hurry, Steve," he said.

Steve followed, his feet slipping on the slimy, moss-covered rock.

"Pull her up now," Pitch said.

Together they lifted the prow out of the water and then swung the dory sideways until she was directly behind, and protected by, the larger rock. That done, they sat down quickly beside the dory. For a moment they said nothing, each listening to the heavy thud of waves crashing against the face of the rock.

Finally Pitch asked, "Now what, Steve? It's just about as bad as in the canyon."

"But it's not as smooth nor as steep," Steve pointed out hopefully. "Maybe we can get a foothold some place and be able to climb up."

"It's difficult to tell from here," Pitch said.

Simultaneously they looked in front of them at the low coral rock that stretched before them to the wall. Their first task would be to cross it safely. They waited for the waters to drain from the rock, and saw the green, slippery moss that grew there.

"We'll have to be careful," Pitch cautioned. "Very careful."

Steve's eyes were still fixed upon the rock. He

studied it intently for a few minutes more before suddenly crawling forward on his hands and knees. He pushed away some of the green vegetation, exposing a long uneven niche in the rock. A few feet above it he uncovered another. His eyes followed the indentations up to the small crest of the rock, then he turned to Pitch. "They're almost like steps," he said excitedly. "Do you think the sea could have cut them in the rocks, Pitch?"

"I suppose so," Pitch returned, after studying the niches. "Although they do seem to be about the same distance apart, leading right across. Maybe they even go to the wall."

"It's hard to tell," Steve said, "because the moss covers them so well. If we can find them, they'll give us a little foothold." Steve's hands were on the rock. "Shall we try it now, Pitch?"

Pitch knelt directly behind Steve. "I suppose so," he said hesitantly. "I'll never be more ready than I am now."

They heard a wave strike the face of the rock, then the waters came pouring over the sides, sweeping past them and covering the low rock. They waited until the waters drained from the rock and the way was clear again, then Steve went ahead, followed closely by Pitch.

Steve was in a full crouch, his hands clawing at the rock in front of him until he found the cuts; then he would bring his feet up to them, while his hands moved forward again, searching for the footholds he hoped he'd find beneath the green moss. When he reached the small crest of the rock he started down toward the wall, only a few feet away. It was more difficult finding the cuts now . . . or perhaps there were none, he thought. He stopped looking for them as he heard the next wave crash with a dull thud against the large rock behind him. There were only a few seconds now before the water would sweep over the path he was following. Ahead he saw a long narrow ledge on the wall, a few feet above the rock. He let himself go. Sliding and slipping, he went over the remaining bit of rock until he had reached the wall, then quickly stepped up to the ledge. He no sooner had turned his back to the wall than Pitch was climbing up beside him.

They stood there catching their breath while the wave covered the rock, swept up to their feet, then receded, rolling seaward.

"It could have been worse," Steve said encouragingly.

"Yes. Yes, I suppose so," Pitch said slowly. Then he turned and looked at the ledge running along the wall. "We can't just stand here, Steve, so let's see where this goes. If it comes to nothing we'll just have to call it quits and go back again."

Moving slowly, Steve sidestepped along the

narrow ledge. He had gone about thirty yards when the ledge ended abruptly at a shallow cleft in the rock.

Steve and Pitch stood there, saying nothing, their eyes taking in the smooth stone on either side of them. Overhead, the cleft rose about fifty feet. Pitch moved off the ledge and into the cleft beside Steve; there was just enough room for both of them. "Well, this seems to be the end," Pitch said dismally. "There's no place to go from here."

Steve hated to turn back now, for there was no other way, he knew, of setting foot onto this part of the island. But Pitch was right . . . there was no place to go from here. No place but up.

Pitch had moved back to the ledge, and Steve pushed his foot against the wall of the cleft. As he did so he could feel a small indentation in the rock. He swept his foot along it, scattering the small stones that lay there. He could see it clearly now; the indentation was worn almost smooth, but it was still very much like the uneven cuts in the rock they had just climbed over. He glanced at a point a few feet above the first cut; then, quickly, he leaned forward, his fingers finding another niche in the stone wall. Looking above his head, he saw several more slight indentations; but whether or not they went all the way up the wall he could not tell, for they were too shallow to be seen from any distance.

Pitch had turned away from him, but Steve

excitedly called him back. Pointing to the lowest niche in the wall, he said, "Look, Pitch! Here are those cuts again."

Crouching down beside Steve, Pitch felt the cuts; then after Steve had shown him the others, he said, "They certainly look the same, Steve. But why would anyone . . ."

"Here's why!" Steve said quickly. He braced his back against the wall opposite the cuts, then raised his feet to the first niche. And there he sat, wedged between the walls of the cleft!

"You mean . . ." Pitch began.

Instead of replying, Steve placed one foot in the next cut, then slid his back up the wall until he was still higher above the ground.

Pitch looked up at him in amazement. "Can you come down the same way?" he asked.

"Sure," Steve said, and he slowly made his way back to the ground. "We can do it, Pitch," he said. "We can go right up, as long as those cuts are there to give us a foothold!"

"But do you think they go all the way up, Steve?"

"I'm sure they do. Those cuts were made by someone as a way of getting up from this ledge! Come on, Pitch," Steve said anxiously, "you can easily do it."

Once more Steve was in the cleft, and a few seconds later he was moving slowly up between the walls. Pitch watched him for a few moments, and then, when it was obvious that Steve wasn't going to wait for him or turn back, Pitch hesitantly started up himself. He found it easier than he had expected as long as he kept his back hard against the opposite wall and his feet firmly in the cuts. Soon he was gaining upon Steve, who had to spend time uncovering each cut before going on.

As Steve neared the top he could see the wide ledge above. He pushed himself up the remaining few feet and then crawled out upon it. Pitch was just behind, and Steve reached down to help him up.

They stood there side by side, looking about them. Below was a precipitous drop to the sea, and above another sheer wall of yellow stone. Pitch had begun to shake his head dismally when he saw the square box-shaped stone that rose a few feet above the center of the ledge. "Look here, Steve," he said, running to it.

When Steve joined Pitch, he found him looking down a darkened shaft. The hole was about four feet in area, and the stone about it was squared off at each corner. "Somebody built this," Steve said, looking down into the blackness of the hole. "What is it? Where does it go?"

Pitch was running his hands around the sides. "This isn't stone," he said. "It's a mortar of some kind. See how it crumbles, Steve. I'd say it's hundreds of years old."

"What's the hole for?"

"I don't know for sure. But it could be a ventilation shaft," Pitch returned.

"You mean to tunnels below?" Steve asked. "Tunnels that may lead to the interior of the island?"

"Your guess is as good as mine, Steve," Pitch replied quickly. "We've really stumbled onto something."

Looking down the shaft, Steve said, "How deep do you think it goes, Pitch?"

Pitch looked about the ledge. "If we had something to drop we could tell approximately," he said. They searched the ledge but could find nothing on the bare rock; then Pitch put his hand in his pockets and finally withdrew a long piece of white chalk. "This will do," he said. "I must have picked it up at the customs office when you arrived." Leaning over the shaft, he added, "Listen closely now," and dropped the chalk.

Steve heard Pitch counting to himself as the chalk fell; then came the soft thud as it struck the bottom of the shaft.

Pitch said, "About a hundred feet, Steve, as close as I can figure it."

"The rope could easily do it then," Steve said quickly.

"You mean for us to go down?" Pitch asked, his eyes becoming grave. "You think we should, Steve? We don't know what we'll find below. It might be dangerous."

"We can't stop now," Steve pleaded. "We've been looking for a possible way into the interior. We've found it. We can easily fit into the shaft."

Pitch was silent for a moment; then he said thoughtfully, "And if we find nothing, we can always climb back up the rope. We'll tie it securely about the top of the shaft here." His voice had become eager again.

"Yes," Steve added, "and we'll have our flashlight to use below. We'll have to go back to the dory to get it, and we should get our packs, too. If we find anything and decide to stay, we'll need everything we have with us. We'd better make sure the dory will stay fast as well."

Pitch nodded. "Yes, we'd better, as you say."

But they still stood at the edge of the shaft, looking into the blackness below.

"We found what we were looking for, Pitch."

"Much more, actually," Pitch said slowly. "Much more."

6

Underground World

———

STEVE placed the lid on top of the can of Sterno, extinguishing the flame over which the midday meal had been cooked. Pitch had risen to his feet, wiped his tin plate clean with a paper towel, and walked over to the shaft. He stood looking down for a few minutes, then glanced up at the overcast sky and said, "We're in for some rain, I'm afraid."

Smiling, Steve snapped the lid tightly over the can and placed it inside his pack along with the small folded stove. "It won't bother us, not where we're going," he said.

On the ground about them, besides the shoulder packs, were two coils of rope, one lying on top of the other, and Pitch's pick and shovel, which he had insisted upon bringing along. It had taken them well over an hour to get everything from the dory. They had made their way slowly down the cleft in the wall and along the narrow ledge until they were again facing the sea-swept path to the large rock and the dory lying behind it. Then it was Steve who had insisted upon making the two trips across the low coral rock for the equipment, and Pitch, knowing the boy was surer footed than he, had let him go. On the first trip, Steve had returned with one pack, and on the second he had tied the pick and shovel to the rope so Pitch could haul them across the turbulent waters. Steve had followed with the last pack fastened high upon his shoulders so it would not hinder him as he bent far over on his way across the slippery rock. The rest had been easier, for Pitch had gone up the cleft again and pulled up all the equipment by rope while Steve waited below.

They had then decided to eat, telling each other they were hungry, when actually they weren't. The meal had been unhurried, almost leisurely, until each wondered if the other was deliberately putting off their descent down the shaft.

Steve told himself repeatedly that there was nothing to be frightened about. He really wasn't frightened. Well, perhaps just a little, he admitted to himself. There was always something frightening in the unknown. They didn't know where the shaft led, if indeed it was a shaft as Pitch thought. The darkness below made it worse. If it were light, it would be different. One could do all sorts of things in the daylight. That's why everything else they'd done today was different from what faced them now. Yet, Steve argued with himself, wouldn't it be much easier than climbing over the slippery rock and scaling the cleft? All they had to do now was to slide down a rope. But it was black, terrifyingly black below . . . and that made all the difference in the world.

Pitch left the shaft and walked toward him. There was nothing else to do now. There was no more equipment to be brought up to the ledge. They'd eaten. Everything was put away. They couldn't just sit there. It would be raining soon.

Pitch started to say something, paused to clear his throat, then began all over again. "Shall we lower the packs?"

"We'd better go down first and see what's there," Steve said slowly. "No sense lowering the stuff if we're not going to stay. We'd just have to haul it up again."

Pitch nodded without saying anything. After a few minutes, he picked up one of the ropes and went over to the shaft. Steve followed.

Pitch drew the rope around the top of the shaft, tied one end, then pulled hard, tightening the knot. Satisfied that it wouldn't slip, he threw the coil down the shaft. The rope disappeared into the darkness of the hole, uncoiling like a brown snake until the end struck the bottom with a dull thud.

"At least we know the rope reaches the bottom," Pitch said.

Steve said quietly, "I'll go down now, and when I get to the bottom I'll let you know whether to lower the packs or not." He reached for the flashlight Pitch was holding in his hand.

"I'm going first," Pitch said, just as quietly as Steve.

"But it's easier for . . ." Steve began.

Pitch already had hold of the rope and one foot was resting on the edge of the shaft.

"Pitch, it's so much easier for me to climb up, if it's necessary. I can make it fast, Pitch!"

Straddling a side of the shaft, Pitch placed the flashlight in his pocket and carefully buttoned the pocket flap over it. "Someone has to be in charge of an expedition like this," he said with feigned lightness. "And because of my age I'm electing myself." He looked up at Steve. "There's really nothing to it, you know. We've gone through much worse today."

Pitch's hands tightened about the rope as he slid into the shaft and began working his way down, his feet pressed stiffly against the wall. Steve watched him until he could no longer see the top of Pitch's white sun helmet, and he found himself thinking how silly it was for Pitch to be wearing his helmet when he was going a hundred feet or more under the ground. Taking off his own helmet, he flung it to one side.

For a few minutes, Steve could hear the sound of

Pitch's feet scraping the wall. The rope was taut. Fingering it, Steve waited until the sounds from Pitch no longer reached his ears and the rope had lost its tautness. He knew then that Pitch had reached the bottom of the shaft. "Pitch! Pitch! Are you all right?"

There were a few seconds of frightening, agonizing silence, then Pitch's voice came up the shaft so suddenly that the sound burst upon Steve's ears. "I'm all right. It's a tunnel, just as we thought, Steve. I'm going to look around."

"Pitch! You'd better wait," Steve called. But as the echo died away, there was only deadening silence within the shaft.

Hanging over the side, Steve waited. Every minute seemed an hour. His thin lips were set, his dark eyes stared into the blackness below. If anything happens to Pitch, he thought . . . If anything happens . . .

Then Pitch's voice came up the shaft again. "Come down, Steve," he called excitedly. "I've really found something."

Steve had one leg inside the shaft when he saw the packs lying on the ground. "Pitch!" he shouted. "What about the packs? Shall I lower them down first? Are we going to stay?"

"Yes, Steve. Yes, you'd better lower everything down. We can't stop now . . . not now."

Anxious to get below, Steve hurriedly tied the

second coil of rope about the packs and lowered them into the shaft. "Coming down," he called to Pitch. "Watch your head."

When he felt the packs touch the bottom of the shaft, he flung his leg over the side once more. But then he stopped again when he caught sight of Pitch's pick and shovel. Surely Pitch wouldn't have any use for them; they'd been enough of a nuisance already. He grabbed hold of the rope to let himself down, then hesitated again. Finally he called down the shaft, "How about the pick and shovel? Do you want them, too?"

"Oh, yes, Steve," came the quick reply. "I want them very much."

Shaking his head, Steve climbed out of the shaft and pulled up the second rope. When he had drawn it to the top, he tied the pick and shovel to it and lowered away. As soon as he heard the implements strike bottom, he was on his way down the shaft.

He lowered himself quickly, the rope sliding between his hands. The darkness closed in about him, and a strong current of air from above beat upon his head. He took one quick look up at the sky and saw the heavy gray clouds overhead; then he turned away. He didn't have far to go when Pitch flashed the light upon him, then switched it off again. Steve figured that Pitch was saving the battery, but he thought it unnecessary since they had brought along four extra batteries.

The light came on again and Steve saw Pitch's face behind the glow as his feet found the stone floor.

"Notice how smooth it is," Pitch said, flashing the light downward. "We're not the first here by any means. Look here, too, Steve."

He flashed the light over the yellow walls on either side of them, and then directed it toward the ceiling, which was so low that the two of them had to stand in a crouched position beneath it. "This tunnel is partly natural in formation, Steve. It could have been cut as far back as the Ice Age, then pushed up by some giant upheaval which took place." Pitch paused, then added with great awe, "But a lot of it has been worked out by hand. Notice the perfect regularity of the cutting on each side and on the ceiling here."

Steve's eyes were following the beam of light. "By whose hands?" he asked.

"The Spaniards, Steve. The Spaniards," Pitch returned quickly. "They probably started work on it early in the sixteenth century and continued for well over a hundred and fifty years . . . until shortly after 1669, I'd say."

"How do you know, Pitch? Why are you so sure it was the Spaniards?"

Without a word Pitch took Steve by the arm and led him up an incline, flashing the light ahead of them. Steve's back was almost touching the low ceiling. His sense of direction told him they were going toward the sea and that they still must be directly beneath the ledge. Suddenly Pitch switched off the light. A few yards ahead, Steve saw three narrow slits of daylight coming through the rock.

Stopping before the slits, Pitch flashed on the light again, and Steve saw that they had reached the end of the tunnel. Pitch stood flat against the wall to enable Steve to get beside him. Two of the slits were on either side of the tunnel and the other was directly between them. They were at eye height and each slit was about three feet deep and a foot wide. But as Steve looked through one of them he saw that the sides of the slit were tapered and that the opening outside was less than an inch wide. Looking through the slit, Steve could see the ocean to the right of the ledge overhead.

"Look through the middle one now," Pitch said.

Through this slit, Steve saw a continuation of the view from the first slit.

"Now the next one," Pitch said.

Curiously, yet suspecting what he'd find, Steve looked through the slit on the far left of the tunnel. Again he saw a continuation of the view from the middle slit; and he also was able to see the large rock behind which the dory still lay, as well as the narrow ledge below that led to the cleft in the wall.

Pitch said, "A man with a gun could cover every possible approach from this point, Steve."

"Then they're gun slits," Steve said quickly.

"Exactly," Pitch replied. "They're wide enough in

here to slip the barrel of a gun through, but the tiny opening on the outside of the wall makes them a very difficult target for anyone firing from the sea."

"And that's what makes you so certain it was the Spaniards who used this tunnel?" Steve asked.

"Who else would have been likely to attack from the sea, Steve? Remember that in those days Spain's armies ruled the New World, but they were. in constant danger of attacks by pirates. I told you," he added, "how Antago was sacked by pirates in 1669. The Spaniards could have had ready just such a place as this to which to flee when they were driven from Antago."

"Then what do you actually think we'll find here, Pitch?" Steve asked excitedly.

"Most anything, Steve. Most anything," Pitch repeated quickly. "Come on." Taking small, hurried steps, he moved back down the tunnel, followed by Steve.

Arriving at the shaft again, they were able to stand upright. They remained there for a few minutes, resting their backs; then Pitch said, "We'd better get on, Steve."

They placed the packs upon their shoulders and as Pitch flung the second coil of rope about his neck, the beam from the flashlight fell upon the pick and shovel.

"You still want to take them along?" Steve asked. "It's going to be trouble enough with just the packs."

Nodding, Pitch said, "I don't dare leave them behind now." Reaching for the shovel, he added, "If you'll just carry the pick, Steve."

With a last look up the shaft at the gray sky, Steve followed Pitch down the tunnel. The descent was not steep, but it seemed never-ending, and soon Steve felt the dull ache in his legs from the stiff, awkward steps he had to take in his crouched position. The light pack became heavier, and the pick he carried was an added weight to his misery.

Suddenly Pitch came to an abrupt stop as the flashlight revealed a sharp angle to the right.

"Another tunnel," Pitch said.

"But we should keep going down, the way we're doing," Steve returned. "This other tunnel probably only goes to another spot along the sea."

"I know," Pitch said. "But I was thinking of our return trip. We want to make sure that we have no trouble getting back to our rope. We mustn't get lost. If only we had something to mark our way . . ."

"The chalk!" Steve said quickly. "You dropped it down the shaft. We could mark our way with that."

"Just the thing, Steve."

"I'll get it."

Pitch handed over the flashlight to Steve, who removed his pack and then went back up the tunnel. Sitting down on the ground, Pitch watched as the light moved along to the steady sound of Steve's footsteps. A little while later, the light flashed downward and Pitch knew that Steve had arrived back at the shaft. The light bobbed around the ground, then was turned in Pitch's direction again.

"I've got it, Pitch!" Steve called down the tunnel.

Back with Pitch, Steve sat down and rested while his friend marked a large arrow on the wall of the tunnel, pointing in the direction of the shaft.

"We can't miss it now," Pitch said. "And we'll do the same each time we come to another tunnel."

Soon they were on their way again, stopping only when they found other tunnels diverging from the one they were following. "This place is a maze," Pitch said after a while. "We'd never have found our way back without the chalk marks."

Downward, ever downward they went, their footsteps beginning to drag, their cramped muscles sore and painful. They began to stop more often, even when they did not come upon other passage-ways. They found, too, that they were too tired to talk, so they sat quietly beside each other during their frequent rests.

Rubbing his legs, Steve breathed deeply and wondered that the air was still so fresh and clean. There must be many ventilation shafts up the other tunnels, he decided, yet he and Pitch had not come across any on their way down. They must be hundreds of feet below the surface of the ground and far into the interior of Azul Island. Well, he asked himself, wasn't that what he wanted? No, not quite . . . because when he started he was looking for a horse. Now he found himself in a catacomb, almost a lost world! Yes, but they go together, his mind insisted. If, as Pitch figured, the Spanish Conquistadores were responsible for the building of these tunnels, they also were responsible for the stallion on the cliff. Only those who knew the secrets of this underground world could have gotten a horse into the interior of Azul Island!

Steve continued thinking about the horse on the cliff as he rose and followed Pitch down the tunnel. A horse needed grazing land, so surely these tunnels had to lead to the surface. Surely there had to be more than just these passages running through the yellow rock. A horse couldn't live underground. But this tunnel through which they were traveling continued to go ever downward. Was it the wrong tunnel? Should they have taken one of the others? Of all the many tunnels was there only one that led to the surface? Were they to spend days groping around behind the beam of their flashlight, as they were doing now? Were they . . .

Pitch came to a sudden stop and Steve bumped into him. "What is it, Pitch?" And although Steve's voice was little more than an anxious whisper, it echoed loudly through the tunnel.

Without saying a word, Pitch turned the beam of light to the right. Steve fully expected to see another tunnel, but instead he saw a high natural cleavage in the stone. Then Pitch flashed the light inside over a long rectangular room with a jagged ceiling all of six feet high. They entered the door, straightening their backs and glorying in the feeling of being able to stand upright again.

Pitch slowly turned the flashlight over the walls and ceiling. They saw the ventilation shaft in the middle of the chamber. Then Pitch brought the light down a little lower. There, in front of their eyes, was a long table of heavy wood!

Running forward, Pitch stood before the table. The flashlight's beam moved over a surface heavily laden with a fine gray dust.

"What's that behind the table?" Steve asked suddenly.

Pitch turned the flashlight on the object on the floor, and they both saw the overturned chair. But their eyes left it for the carved crest and lettering upon the wall behind it.

They rounded the table quickly, Pitch holding the flashlight close to the wall. Half obliterated with age, but still faintly seen, was the outline of a scroll, in the center of which they made out the figure of a lion standing upon his hind legs and holding a small bird clutched between his paws.

79

"A coat of arms," Pitch said huskily

"A coat of arms," Pitch said huskily.

The lettering beneath the crest was in Spanish and only the top two lines could be made out:

$$1669 \text{ AÑOS}$$
$$\text{AQUÍ EL CAPITAN RA} \dots$$

His voice still heavy with emotion, Pitch translated: "In the year 1669. Here Captain . . ." He turned to Steve. "That's the year the Spaniards were driven from Antago by the pirates," he said quickly. "Steve! This proves I'm right! This is a fort to which the Spaniards fled after leaving Antago!"

In his excitement Pitch had directed the flashlight's beam from the wall to the opposite side of the room, and there they saw another great split in the wall, leading to a chamber beyond. "Look, Steve!" Pitch shouted. "Another room!"

Pitch ran around the table toward the doorway. He was nearing the center of the room when suddenly there was the sharp clanking of metal against stone. Steve caught a glimpse of the shovel as Pitch's foot sent it wildly across the room. Then Pitch fell, and the flashlight went out to the sound of splintering glass. Stumbling against the table in the darkness, Steve groped his way forward, trying to find Pitch.

7

Lost!

_____

IN THE darkness, Steve could make out the dim square of light beneath the ventilation shaft. Pitch's legs were within this patch of light, but the rest of his body was enveloped in the darkness of the chamber.

As Steve reached him, Pitch was drawing one leg up to a kneeling position.

"Pitch! Are you all right?"

There was a groan more of disgust than agony as Pitch said, "Got the wind knocked out of me. But the flash, Steve! Where is it? Is it broken?"

They found it by groping in the dark, running their frantic hands across the cold, smooth stone. They took one look at it in the dim light of the shaft and knew immediately that it was hopeless to think it would ever work again. The end had been driven hard against the stone; there was no lens, no bulb, nothing but a battered, twisted piece of metal.

"Maybe it'll work, Pitch. We've got other bulbs. We can try."

Shaking his head, Pitch muttered, "Sure we've got more bulbs. More batteries, too. But not another flash. We haven't a chance."

Steve was making his way toward where they'd left the packs when he heard Pitch mutter angrily, almost to himself, "What a numbskull I am! What a stupid fool not to have brought another flash along!"

After finding the packs, Steve pulled them across toward Pitch. "You didn't know we were going to go through this," he said. "I should have thought of another flash too. It's my fault as much as yours."

They found they couldn't even get the bulbs into the wrenched socket.

Looking into the darkness, Pitch said, "A nice mess. Luckily, we have plenty of matches and we shouldn't have too much trouble getting back . . . if we're careful."

"Back," slowly repeated Steve. "Yes, I guess we do have to go back."

"There's no other choice," Pitch said. "We could roam through these tunnels for a long time, I'm afraid, without finding our way to whatever it is that's at the end of them. If there is an end to them," he added grudgingly.

Steve didn't say anything.

"We'll have to go back to Antago to get another flash, and then we can return," Pitch went on. "We've licked the hardest part, Steve. It'll only mean losing a couple of days, and we have plenty of time."

Plenty of time. No, Steve thought, I don't have plenty of time at all. I have two weeks before going home. Two days mean a lot to me. And we've gone through so much to turn back. We may be very near the end of the tunnel now, he told himself hopefully. It couldn't just go on and on! Yet he wondered if it did. Did this tunnel only lead to others that would take them still deeper within the yellow stone of Azul Island? What then? The matches soon would be gone. Then there never would be a chance of finding their way back.

"I guess you're right, Pitch," he said finally. "We have no choice but to go back."

Standing up, Pitch put his pack upon his shoulders. "We'd better take them along," he said, "just in case . . ."

Pitch had left his sentence unfinished, but Steve knew perfectly well what he had meant to say. *Just in case they missed the chalked arrows. Just in case they got lost!*

Pitch had the large box of matches in his hand. "We really shouldn't have any trouble," he said, but there was a grimness to his voice that belied his light tone. "We'll strike a match every fifty yards or so as we go along. There should be plenty to last. And I have another box if we need them," he added quickly. "Ready, Steve?"

Hooking the pack upon his shoulders and picking up the rope Pitch had had about his neck when he fell, Steve replied, "Okay, Pitch."

They had walked only a few paces across the room when Pitch struck the first match. In its glow they saw the pick and shovel. "We'll leave them behind this time," Pitch said.

Before the light dimmed, they both turned toward the cleavage in the wall they had seen a few minutes earlier. "I'd just like to take a look inside," Pitch said. "We can spare the match."

As the match burned out Steve followed Pitch, his hand upon Pitch's shoulder. Their fingers touched the wall and felt along it to the opening they were seeking.

"Now," Pitch said, lighting another match.

They stood just within the room, but as the match flared, then steadied, they backed away a pace, startled at what they saw before them. It was a long, narrow room with a ceiling no higher than the tunnel. Along the bottom of the wall were iron rings and fastened to each was a short chain . . . chains that were still about bones that once had been the wrists of many men. Grotesquely, their skeletons still remained sitting upright, their white skulls leaning wearily against the wall. And with the flickering of the match they seemed to move horribly.

85

Pitch dropped the match and, frantically, he and Steve groped their way through the darkness of the outer chamber until their fingers found the opening leading to the tunnel. Outside they hurriedly turned left, knowing that was the direction from which they had come. They ran until their legs gave way beneath them, then slipped wearily to the floor and lay there in the darkness.

It was a few minutes before Pitch struck a match, and within its glow their faces were still white and taut.

Pitch said almost angrily, "We were very silly to run. We have to be more careful or we'll lose our way."

Yes, Steve admitted to himself, it had been silly to run as they had done. Yet one often did things without thinking. This had been one of those times. He was not ashamed, for he knew that many men braver than he or Pitch would have had a similar reaction to the horrible sight of men who centuries ago had died a living death, chained to the walls of a black pit hundreds of feet beneath the ground.

Soon they started again and found that going up the tunnel was easier on their legs than coming down. At regular intervals Pitch would light a match, and from its glow they would look ahead for the other tunnels they had passed on their way down. Then, as the light flickered and died, they would walk forward again until they came to what they figured had been the range of their last light. They would stop then to light another match before going on.

After more than half an hour Pitch said gravely, "Something must be wrong, Steve. I'm certain we should have run across other tunnels before this. I remember marking one just fifteen minutes or so before we reached the chamber on our way down."

"Yes," Steve admitted slowly, "I know you did. Do you think we could have taken another tunnel somewhere along the line? We must have run a hundred yards before we lit our first match."

"I would say it was more like three hundred yards before we stopped running," Pitch returned.

"It couldn't have been, Pitch . . ." Steve stopped, suddenly realizing that probably neither of them was right. In the darkness they could have run from fifty to five hundred yards for all they knew. Fright did that to a person. "We'd better turn back then," he said aloud.

"Yes, we'd better." Pitch made no effort to keep the concern from his voice. They both were aware of the consequences of getting lost.

As they started back down the tunnel Pitch said, "You keep a hand on the right wall when we go along in the dark, Steve. I'll keep mine on the left wall; that way we won't slip by any tunnels that may converge with this one. If there's a break, stop . . . and I'll do the same."

They had walked along for about half an hour

when suddenly Steve's hand encountered nothing but air. "Wait, Pitch!" he called.

Pitch struck a match and they saw another tunnel. "You see we missed this on the way up," he said. Eagerly they looked for a large white arrow, but found none. "Obviously," Pitch continued dismally, "we didn't come down either one of these tunnels on our way to the chamber or there would be an arrow on one of them."

"Then which one did we just come up?" Steve asked anxiously. "Which one goes back to the chamber?"

Pitch didn't answer. And Steve couldn't help him. They simply couldn't tell, for both tunnels went downward and at this point they came together in a V-shape.

"One's as good as another," Steve said grimly. "Let's take our pick, Pitch."

Pitch's round face was grim and his pale blue eyes were but slits in the light of the burning match. "Don't worry, Steve. We've got plenty of matches. We'll find our way out."

But still they stood before the two tunnels, neither caring to make the decision. They knew that only one tunnel went back to the chamber where they'd have a chance of picking up the arrows again.

"We could separate," Steve suggested. "You take one tunnel and I the other. We'll come back after going a short way."

"A short way wouldn't do it," Pitch protested. "We must be all of half an hour from the chamber. No, Steve, we'd better stick together. We need each other now."

"Then let's go to the right," Steve suggested quickly. "The right way could be right," he added without smiling.

Pitch nodded, and once again they made their way downward. They had traveled for about fifteen minutes when the burning match disclosed another tunnel, going still farther to the right.

"This is the end," Pitch said dismally. "We may have been lucky enough to guess correctly the first time, but doing it again is asking too much of luck."

Steve said slowly, "Will it be to the right or the left or back?"

They stood there long after the match had burned out, neither saying a word. Finally Pitch struck another match, and in the light their faces were haggard and old, far beyond their years. When the match burned out, Pitch took Steve by the arm and led him down the tunnel to the right.

They went along for an hour, coming across several more tunnels, and always they went to the right without stopping, without talking. It didn't matter to them which direction they took now, for they were fully convinced they weren't going to find their way back to the chamber. They still looked hopefully for the chalked arrows each time they came to another tunnel, but they really didn't expect to find them either now.

After a while their stops to rest became more frequent, for they were conserving their energy. And the intervals between the striking of matches were longer, for the matches too had to be conserved. They needed the matches more than ever now. Not so much for showing them their way, as for the warmth they gave, a spiritual warmth that penetrated deeper and deeper into their very souls as they went along. Each time a match was struck they looked more eagerly at each other, as though they had not seen one another for a long, long time. Darkness did that to people. One could take only so much of darkness. Their hands were raw from constant contact with the uneven wall, but they did not know they bled. Their cramped muscles no longer pained them; it was as though they had always walked in this hunched position, and always down, down. Was there no end to this descent? they asked themselves over and over again. Did it end nowhere? . . . Yet the air remained fresh. It had been almost an hour since they had last seen a ventilation shaft running hundreds and hundreds of feet up to the surface. They had stood beneath it a long time, gazing fixedly at the small patch of blue sky above. Yes, it was blue now instead of gray. They had noticed that immediately. The rain must have come and gone, then. They had talked about it at length before giving up their patch of blue for the blackness ahead.

Much later they came to another tunnel, where Pitch slipped to the floor, saying, "I'm almost whipped, Steve. I'd like to rest a while."

Slowly Steve stretched out on the floor behind him, too tired to remove his pack. "We'll rest, Pitch . . . as you say. Later we'll have something to eat. We'll feel better then . . . much better."

He closed his eyes and thought of the two of them cooking their meal down here. Maybe it would be a record of some kind. "The World's Finest Underground Meal" . . . that's the way they'd advertise it, he thought morosely. It would make a good story to tell the fellows back home. Yes, he'd say, we had chipped beef and beans cooked just right over our Sterno stove. Steve opened his eyes as he thought of the can of Sterno. "Pitch," he said slowly, "how many cans of Sterno did we bring along?"

"About eight." Pitch spoke with an effort; then Steve heard him chuckle. "But I'd figured on using driftwood to cook most of our meals. That's a laugh, isn't it? Lots of driftwood down here, all right. Just bundles of it."

"At least we can use the Sterno when we're getting low on matches," Steve said thoughtfully. "It's too bad we didn't think to use a can when we first started back. We wouldn't have lost our way then."

As Steve finished, Pitch's steady breathing reached his ears. It was good that Pitch was sleeping, he thought. They both needed sleep. It probably wasn't even dark outside yet. But it didn't matter here. Down here one didn't have to wait for night to fall before going to sleep. It was always night here.

It could have been a minute or hours that Steve slept when suddenly he became conscious of a low steady hum in his ears. He thought it was Pitch's breathing until he realized there was no break in the sound, no interval as there would be between the deep breaths of a sleeping man. Steve opened his eyes. The hum was very low yet very distinct. He tried to place the sound; it was something he should know. It came from the tunnel to the right.

"Pitch!"

Steve listened again. It was still there, low and never-ending.

"Pitch!"

He was beginning to wonder if he actually did hear anything. He wanted somebody else to hear it. Pitch had to hear it!

"Pitch!" Frantically Steve climbed to his feet and shook Pitch's leg until he awakened.

"Listen, Pitch! Do you hear it?"

Pitch sat up but said nothing.

The low humming swept through Steve's ears until he couldn't stand Pitch's silence any longer. "You hear it, Pitch! You do hear it, don't you?" His voice was pleading, entreating.

"I think I hear something," Pitch said slowly. "I'm not quite sure, though. My ears . . ."

"Is it a low, humming sound, Pitch? Do you think it might get louder if we walked down that tunnel to the right?" Steve was almost in a frenzy. He wished he could see Pitch. He would be able to tell by his eyes whether or not Pitch was saying he *did* hear something just to agree with him. But he couldn't see Pitch.

"Steve!" Pitch's voice was raised, excited. "I do hear it now. It sounds almost like water . . . rushing water!"

"Yes, that's it!" Steve yelled, moving past Pitch. "It's a stream!" He was already on his way down the tunnel when Pitch rose from the floor and hurriedly followed.

Steve was in a half-run when his outstretched hands banged against a wall in front of him. "A match, Pitch. Quick!" he cried.

Striking a match, Pitch moved up toward Steve. Ahead they saw that the tunnel took a sharp right-angle turn to a short flight of steps cut in the stone. Eagerly they rushed up the steps, and before the lighted match had gone out completely they saw that the tunnel now ran up instead of down.

Then it was dark again.

"Careful," Pitch warned. "Let's go slowly now."

Steve went forward, his head and shoulders down as before, his skinned hands trailing the walls on either side of him. The low, humming sound became louder. It rushed and roared in his ears. His half-steps came faster until he was running again.

"Slower, Steve! You're going much too fast," Pitch warned from behind. "Stop, and we'll light another match now."

In the light of the burning match, they saw that the tunnel continued to lead upward. Steve plunged forward. After the light died out, he had gone only a few yards when his right shoulder crashed heavily against stone. He reeled back from the force of the impact, falling at Pitch's feet.

Quickly Pitch struck another match and bent down toward Steve. The worry in his eyes turned to anger when he saw that Steve was all right and climbing to his knees. "You fool, Steve!" he shouted. "You can't go plunging through this tunnel. You should know that by now!" Then the anger left his voice as he said, "I'll go first hereafter, Steve. I don't want you to get hurt."

Steve nodded, but he was only conscious of the ever-increasing roar ahead of them. "We must be very close to it now," he said.

The tunnel took a sharp turn to the left this time, and Pitch struck another match. Ahead, the tunnel continued to lead upward, but Pitch too knew they were almost at the end. The roar had become the distant sound of rushing water. They moved forward, with Pitch striking matches more frequently than before.

Soon they noticed that the ceiling of the tunnel was gradually becoming higher and they were able slowly to straighten their backs until finally they were standing upright for the first time since they had left the chamber.

Pitch struck another match, and this time they saw the waters of a very narrow but fast-flowing stream plunging directly across their path. They moved forward. The tunnel came to an end at a doorway leading to a high natural cut in the rocks through which the underground stream flowed. It came from their right, rushing past them and continuing downward. Along the stream a narrow path had been cut in the stone.

Turning to Pitch, Steve asked anxiously, "Shall we go down or up the stream?"

Pitch had bent down to the water and was tasting it. "Fresh water," he announced.

Steve drank with him, then said, "I think we should follow the stream down, don't you, Pitch? It has to lead somewhere."

"I think we should, Steve."

Striking another match, they walked cautiously

along the stream. They had gone only a short distance when Steve said quickly, "I'd swear it's getting lighter, Pitch. Don't you notice it?"

"It doesn't seem to be quite so dark," Pitch agreed cautiously.

They struck another match and saw the gradual curve in the course of the stream. While the match burned they walked quickly forward and then slowed down as the light flickered and went out.

The burned match dropped from Pitch's fingers as he grabbed hold of Steve's arm. Ahead of them the blackness of the curving stream gave way to a dim gray light. They rushed forward, needing no burning match to guide their running feet. Rounding the curve, they came to an abrupt stop as they saw a large opening in the rocks through which came the last rays of the setting sun.

They stood there quietly, neither of them saying a word. And when they walked forward again their steps were unhurried as though each was experiencing an emotion he wanted to prolong. For they were walking from the fear of death into the light of the living.

The roar of the stream became louder but they did not hear it; their dazed eyes were focused upon the blue sky ahead. It wasn't until they stood in the great opening in the yellow rock that they saw the water pouring in a silken sheet of white, crashing far down onto the rocks of a large pool two hundred feet or more below them. And stretched before their eyes, as far ahead as they could see, was a long valley within the yellow walls of Azul Island!

"A lost valley," Pitch said unbelievingly. "A lost world!"

But Pitch's words went unheard by Steve. His eyes were fixed upon the shadows to the left of the pool below them. He watched for a few minutes, then his hand tightened about Pitch's arm. For grazing below was a large band of horses, their long tails touching the ground and their small heads stretched forward as they cropped the blue-green grass. Steve's breath came short at the sight of them; then his breathing seemed to stop altogether. Leaving the herd, moving from shadow to sun, stepped the giant stallion of the cliff! He walked toward the pool, his proud head raised high, his muscles moving easily beneath sleek skin. The sun's rays caught at his chestnut coat, turning it into the glowing red of fire.

Under his breath, Steve murmured, *"Flame!"*

8

Fight of the Stallions

THEY stood there for a while in silent awe and
wonder at the scene below them. Steve's eyes
never left the red stallion as he stretched his long
neck in a graceful arc to the water. But Pitch's gaze
turned from the horses to the valley carpeted with the
short, thick, bluish-green grass. He followed it with
his eyes as far ahead as he could see, then looked
over the rolling land that led to the yellow walls
rising high about the valley. There the grass grew tall
and had the appearance of young, green cane. It bent
slightly in the breeze that blew down the valley from
the east. As he looked, the shadows of the walls
lengthened until they reached the floor of the valley,
where suddenly they turned from the dark ominous
black of night to an almost brilliant blue. Pitch
grabbed Steve's arm. "Blue as blue can be, Steve," he
said slowly. "Blue Valley."

The boy looked over at the shadows that had picked up the blue in the grass. "That's where the island gets its name then, Pitch. Azul means blue in Spanish. Blue Island. Blue Valley, as you say." But then his eyes went back to the stallion, who had finished drinking and now stood at gaze, his head moving slowly from side to side. "Let's get closer, Pitch," Steve said. "I want to get closer to them."

Slowly they made their way down the steps cut in the rock until they had almost reached the valley floor; then they came upon a large cave.

"We can set up camp here, Steve," Pitch said. "We're near water. It's everything we need. Just think, Steve," he continued more slowly, "the last persons who lived in that cave were the Conquistadores."

But Steve had turned away from the cave and was again looking at the horses grazing but a short distance away. He took off his pack, letting it slide to the ground, but he didn't follow Pitch into the cave.

His eyes devoured the red stallion, as though to fix him forever in his memory. Yet he had always known this horse. He had looked upon him many times as he was doing now. So he wasn't surprised to see the small, arrogant head with the large eyes set low in the wide and prominent forehead. It was the head of an Arabian, as he knew it would be.

Still in the sun, the red stallion continued to stand at gaze with only his head moving slowly, watch-

99

fully. He was like a giant statue. Steve's eyes moved over every inch of him. He watched the alert, shifting gaze of the stallion, then studied the wedge-shaped head and the small ears now pricked forward until they almost came to a point at the tips. The stallion's head was raised high, yet set at an angle, accentuating the high curve at the crest of his long neck. The length of his back, along with his large size, made it apparent to Steve that he was not a pure-blooded Arabian. Yet Steve knew, from the red stallion's head and neck, from the well-muscled withers, chest and shoulders, from the unusually long quarters and strong legs, that there was a prepon-derance of Arabian blood in this horse.

The red stallion moved; tall and long-limbed he trotted, his tail flowing behind him and his heavy mane sweeping lightly in the breeze. After a short distance he came to an abrupt stop, his gaze still shifting about the valley floor to the west, his ears alert.

Steve too turned his gaze down the valley, but he saw nothing in the dim, fading light of sunset. Still, he knew from the red stallion's actions that he was uneasy. And whatever it was that bothered him was downwind, so the breeze could not bring any scent to his nostrils. He was not frightened, Steve decided, only cautious.

The thirty-odd mares and their long-legged foals were still grazing without so much as a glance at their leader. They were not restless and Steve knew that only a signal of danger from the red stallion would make them abandon their grazing. Yet what had these horses to fear in this lovely, serene valley? Few animals dangerous to them would be on the island. And no animal could withstand the powerful, crushing hoofs of their angered leader.

Steve was watching the band, thinking how little they resembled the small, wiry horses on the plain outside the walls, when Pitch joined him.

"Steve," Pitch said excitedly, "look what I found!" He held an iron spur with a sharp-pointed rowel at the end of it.

Taking the spur from Pitch, Steve ran his fingertips over the spike-wheeled rowel, thinking of the damage it could do to a horse when it was on the heel of a vicious rider.

Pitch said almost reverently, "It's nearly three hundred years old, Steve. Think of it! And there's a heavy wooden table in the cave. There are a couple of chairs, too," he went on quickly. "I'm sure we'll find other caves like this one and probably many other historical relics!"

"But Pitch . . ." Steve's voice was a little annoyed as he turned to his friend. "Why be bothered by relics when . . ." He stopped as he saw the eagerness leave Pitch's eyes. "I mean," he went on, his voice gentler, "those horses down there . . . they're alive, Pitch!" His eyes pleaded with his friend. "And they, or rather their ancestors, were left behind by the Spaniards too. Think of it, Pitch! Look at them!" Steve's voice was raised as he gestured in the direction of the horses. "They're nothing like the horses on the plain."

Pitch was now close beside him. "No," he admitted, "they're not. But don't you think it's because conditions are so much better here, Steve? There's plenty of good grass, water, and the walls protect them from the wind."

Steve shook his head. "No, Pitch. It isn't that at all. These horses have the breeding. I'm convinced that the Conquistadores brought only their finest horses to this valley, and that those on the outside were pack horses or of a cross breed which didn't work out for them."

"You might be right," Pitch said. "I've never seen such beautiful animals and, certainly, never any like that red stallion." He stopped abruptly, turning to Steve, his eyes searching. "Red stallion . . ." he repeated slowly. Then, although he said nothing more, Steve knew Pitch was thinking of Flame and the story he had told him the night before.

Their eyes went back to the red leader as he continued moving uneasily away from his band.

It was Steve who directed Pitch's attention to the band once more. "They all have Arabian blood in them, Pitch. Notice their wedge-shaped heads." And then Steve went on to point out every physical characteristic of the Arabian that he had observed in the horses. He concluded by saying, "They're the same horses the Conquistadores rode centuries ago, Pitch. Maybe even better with their inbreeding and the fact that only the finest and strongest stallion could survive in this small valley. It's his blood that makes them what they are! Look for yourself, Pitch. The red stallion is king of this band and sire of all those long-legged foals running around. They have his blood, and the finest and strongest of the colts will one day take his place." Steve's voice was so low that it almost seemed as though he were talking for his own benefit.

But Pitch had been listening, for he said, "But all this inbreeding, Steve. I don't understand how there could have been so much of it during all these years and still leave the horses with what good qualities they had at the beginning. Of course, I'm a green-horn . . ."

"I only know what I've read, Pitch," Steve said seriously. "And it's a cinch no one has ever known of a band of horses left to themselves for centuries, as these have been, so your opinion is as good as anyone else's. But I've read," he went on, "that inbreeding is perfectly all right if the horses are of the purest blood and don't have any bad traits or weaknesses; because if they do, the bad traits in both sire and dam show up in the foal worse than ever." Steve paused. "But that hasn't happened here . . . at least, as far as we can tell."

They watched the horses for a few more minutes before Pitch said, "I was thinking of the Arabian blood in these horses, Steve. You know that seems logical to me too, now; because the Arabs invaded Spain in about 700 A.D. They remained in Spain for five hundred years before they were forced out, and I'm sure that by that time their horses had become native to Spain." Pleased with his own reasoning, Pitch looked at the horses with renewed interest.

Steve's eyes were upon the red stallion again. The leader's head had stopped moving back and forth but it was still raised high. Steve saw the quivering of the stallion's nostrils as he sniffed the air. He was suspicious of something, yet he remained amazingly cool. He still gave no signal to his complacent followers. Suddenly he turned to the east, up the valley this time, sniffing again.

Steve turned with him, but the rocky slope on which he and Pitch were camped blocked his view of the valley to the east and behind them. When he looked back again at the red stallion, he saw that the leader was moving still farther to the center of the valley. There was a quickness to his gait that hadn't been there before, yet he did not seem frightened. Finally he came to an abrupt stop, his nostrils blown out. Raising his head still higher, he sniffed suspiciously, then quickly turned his head downwind again.

"Seems he's expecting something," Pitch said huskily.

"From both directions," Steve said. "He's picked up some scent from upwind, yet I'm sure he's heard something down the valley, even though he can't smell anything. Look at those ears, Pitch. He's turned downwind again."

For several minutes the red stallion stood still, facing the valley to the west and ignoring whatever it had been from upwind that had caused him to look in that direction. Now his eyes, alert and blazing, were fixed upon one spot down the valley. His nostrils dilated, and his pricked ears suddenly were pulled back flat against his head. He snorted and then gave a loud, sharp whinny.

There was a sudden movement to the band as they stopped grazing. Short, incessant neighs broke the stillness of the valley. Foals, some graceful, others clumsy, ran to their mothers. The band moved away from the long grass and closer to the center of the valley. Nipping and kicking, the mares directed their foals into the middle of a small, tight ring which they formed, their heads toward center and hindquarters tense and ready to fling strong hoofs at any attacker.

The red stallion stood alone, ready to defend his band. Never once did his head turn in the direction of the ring; he seemed to have eyes only for the danger that threatened from down the valley.

Suddenly Pitch said, "There he is!" A stallion was coming up the valley, followed by five or six mares.

"There's going to be a fight, sure as anything," Pitch said quickly. "There's room for only one leader in this place."

Steve said nothing, but his eyes never left the red stallion. He saw him turn his gaze away from the approaching band and come to rest upon his own. The stallion moved his head slowly, as though there was no hurry now that he had seen his foe. Only once did he move about uneasily and that was when he turned again to the east, sniffing. Steve was convinced then that the stallion was aware of danger from upwind too and that it worried him more than the approaching stallion.

Pitch gripped Steve's arm and instinctively the boy looked at the valley below. The rival stallion had left his mares behind and was loping easily toward the red stallion. Suddenly the valley echoed to his shrill clarion call of challenge. As he drew closer, Steve saw that he was a coal black horse. He noticed too that he was as tall and long-limbed as the red stallion and that he had the same perfectly molded form. He moved gracefully, his long, easy gait never changing, his head still and his ears pricked forward almost to a point.

"He's a beauty," Pitch gasped. "Equally as good as the red stallion. This will be a fight to the death,

Steve! Survival of the fittest! We're going to see it, Steve!"

But Steve wasn't listening. He was staring at the red stallion. To Pitch, to anyone else, it would matter little who won the coming encounter. To anyone else there was little to choose between the two stallions. But Steve thought of the red stallion only as Flame. His Flame! The horse he had found again! He didn't want to lose him now. Flame had to win! If this was to be a battle to the death, he wanted Flame to kill!

The red stallion had made no move toward his foe. He stood there quietly, confidently, as though he knew he was king and any challenger to his throne would have to bring the fight to him. Steve watched, marveling at the red stallion's coolness, yet afraid for him as well. "Flame," he said aloud. "I don't want to lose you now. Get ready for him, Flame. He's coming. Don't underestimate him!"

"Just look at that red horse, Steve!" Pitch's voice was guttural, his words hardly distinguishable. "He's been through this before. He's not scared a bit. He's fought his way to the top and that black stallion is going to have to kill him to take his title away. Look, Steve! You never saw such confidence as that red devil has!"

Pitch's words went unheard by Steve, for the boy saw nothing but Flame, standing there, waiting; heard nothing but the running, steady rhythm of hoofs belonging to a black horse as beautiful, swift and strong as the red stallion. Steve knew that in a little while one of them would be no more. It could end no other way, where there could only be one king. Unashamed, he prayed that Flame would win.

The sound of the running hoofs came ever onward, and still the red stallion didn't move forward. Steve saw him turn his head upwind again as though still wary of something he could not see. The beat of hoofs became louder and Steve was forced to focus his attention on the black stallion. The challenger was now rushing headlong into the encounter, and as he drew closer his gait slowed. He was beautiful and powerful to see, and fear for Flame took hold of Steve as he looked again at the red stallion.

His small, arrogant head had turned away from the east and he now faced the challenger. At a sudden, piercing scream from the black stallion he flattened his ears and shattered the air with his own high-pitched whistle. Then, his ears forward, he moved in a slow but steady gait to meet his opponent.

Within the walled amphitheater of Azul Island, across the short, thick grass and ever-lengthening blue shadows, the two stallions moved toward each other to fight for supremacy of a band whose eyes were turned away from the encounter and who would wait for the stronger of the two to claim them.

Cautiously the stallions ran, their strides of equal length, and the distance between them lessened.

Steve said, "Flame . . ." but it was lost in the loud

screams of both stallions as they met.

They moved deftly on winged hoofs. No longer were they beautiful to see, but two raging furies. Their screams drove the serenity and solitude from the valley, and the yellow walls picked up the heavy thuds of their hoofs on flesh and bone and cast them back into the arena.

For many minutes it went on. Equally fast on their feet, the stallions feinted skillfully until one or the other saw an opening; then there would be the charge of thrashing forefeet or powerful hind legs raised to crash heavily against the attacker.

It was too fast, too terrible to go on very long. Steve saw the dark, bleeding wound on Flame's shoulder where the black stallion's hoofs had found their mark, and he prayed for his horse.

Again and again the stallions lunged at each other, neither showing any signs of retreating. Their screams rent the air, and now blood flowed freely from their bodies. There was no difference in the color of their coats any longer. No difference in ravaging teeth and flying hoofs.

"They'll kill each other," Pitch babbled hysterically.

They were on their hind legs, locked together. Steve knew it had to end now. Neither could stand much more. Both would be killed, as Pitch had said.

The end did come at that moment. It came swiftly, sickeningly. Steve saw the black stallion lunge for

Flame's neck and miss. There was a twisting, turning of bodies as Flame hurled himself on the black stallion's hindquarters. His weight threw the black stallion off balance, for he stumbled, then fell. Flame did not let him get up. Screaming, he brought his driving forefeet down on his opponent. He was still pounding when Steve and Pitch turned away, their faces drained of all color.

They said nothing until the sound of battering hoofs stopped and the air was rent by the shrill whistle of triumph from the red stallion.

"It's over," Pitch said huskily.

Steve nodded without saying anything.

"I hope I never see another," Pitch went on. "It's a terrible . . ."

The valley walls resounded to another shrill scream, and Steve turned quickly to Pitch, who said, "That's his scream again."

"No, it's not," Steve returned grimly. "It didn't sound like him at all."

He forced himself to look again. He saw Flame still standing near the broken and lifeless form of the black stallion. Flame's body was ripped and bleeding, his head turned to the east. Steve looked in that direction, then closed his eyes and wept.

Pitch was beside him. "Steve! What's the matter with you? After all . . ."

Then he too saw the monstrosity of a horse which now stood a few hundred yards from the red stallion.

The two stallions fought for supremacy
of the band

He had come with the falling of the sun behind the walls of Azul Island. In the shadows, his massive body penetrated the darkness like a luminous thing. It was as though he belonged only to the night. He was as grotesquely ugly as the red stallion was beautiful. Thick-bodied, he stood still, waiting . . . waiting as he had done all through the fight of the two stallions. Small, close-set eyes—one blue, the other a white wall-eye—gleamed from his large head, which was black except for the heavy blaze that descended over his wall-eye. His neck was thick and short, as was his body, and black too except for the ghostly streaks of white that ran through it. His mane and tail were white.

Arrogant and ruthless, fearing nothing, he moved toward the red stallion at a walk, hate gleaming in his beady eyes. His heavy ears were pulled back flat against his head, his teeth bared. Suddenly he stopped, with ears pitched forward, and screamed his challenge again. He was the embodiment of ugliness, of viciousness. Only the high crest upon his neck and the high set of his tail gave evidence of the Arabian blood in him.

Pitch turned to Steve and saw that the boy was intent upon the terrible drama unfolding before them. Seeing Steve's grim, taut face, he remembered what the boy had said only a few hours before. *"Inbreeding is perfectly all right if the horses are of the purest blood and don't have any bad traits or weaknesses; because if they do, the bad traits in both sire and dam show up in the foal worse than ever."* And then Steve had added, *"But that hasn't happened here . . ."*

But it has happened, Pitch thought, and that monstrosity is the result. Perhaps the same thing has happened before in all the years these horses have been here, but the bad ones have all been killed off. This time, it may be different . . . very different.

Steve said, "Pitch! Why did it have to happen now? He's not ready to fight again. The Piebald will kill him."

The Piebald. Pitch turned to look at him. So that's what this horse with the weird black-and-white markings was called. He came closer, moving faster now, galloping, plunging heavily forward.

Steve watched Flame's every move. His red coat, wet and dark from blood and sweat, was pitiful to see. A little unsteadily, Flame moved away from the dead stallion at his feet. Then he screamed and ran forward, his disheveled head held high, his large eyes blazing with hate.

Again the valley echoed to pounding hoofs over soft-carpeted earth. Swift, light and cautious were the strides of the red stallion. Heavy, plunging and confident were those of the Piebald. The heads of both were raised high; one was small, sensitive and intelligent; the other, large and grotesquely ugly with bright eyes too small and set too close. Each stride brought them closer: a burly, powerful outcast—the product of a cruel twist of Fate—and a long-limbed stallion, graceful, swift and strong, a superb creation.

Steve watched with dull, pained eyes. His desire to see the red stallion win went far beyond his love for Flame; for he knew that if the red stallion won, it would mean more horses like him in the years to come. If he lost, it meant the end of this breed of horse, because the Piebald's blood would flow into the small band. The result would be misfits and monstrosities like him.

His heavy gait unchanging, the Piebald charged the red stallion, who screamed and rose to meet him. There was the hard, wrenching crack of bodies, the raking of teeth, and over it all their terrible screams.

Skillfully the red stallion moved to one side of the Piebald, never underestimating the strength in his opponent's burly body. He darted in with bared teeth and battering forefeet, never staying too long, never giving the Piebald the opportunity of using his heavier weight to his advantage.

For many minutes it went on that way, with the Piebald still confident and awaiting his chance to close in upon his elusive enemy. And soon the red stallion moved away less quickly and the infighting of bared teeth and flying hoofs became more furious.

"Keep away from him, Flame! Keep away!" Steve wanted to shout, but no words came from his lips.

Pitch said, "He's licked! He's too far gone to keep

The end of the fight came quickly

away any longer! He was licked before the fight started!"

They were locked together now, two raging devils with battering hoofs and gleaming teeth. Steve knew that this had to be the end, and he was deathly afraid for his horse. He saw the Piebald wheel, sending his hind legs heavily against the red stallion's shoulder. He heard Flame scream, no longer in fury but in terrible pain. He saw his horse stumble, and then the Piebald was hurling himself upon Flame's hindquarters. Steve knew that it was time for him to look away, but he found he couldn't.

The end of the fight came quickly. Still screaming, the red stallion moved with a sudden, frantic burst of his old speed, avoiding the thrashing forefeet of the Piebald.

Flame had escaped death by only a fraction of a second. He had put off the end, but only momentarily. With grim realization of what the outcome had to be, Steve awaited the red stallion's return lunge at the Piebald.

But there was no charge by Flame, no wheeling to move quickly into position to renew the battle. Instead, the red stallion was running with faltering strides down the valley floor. Behind him the Piebald stood still, his large head raised high; then his scream of triumph rang through the valley, echoing to the broken rhythm of Flame's running hoofs.

9

The Piebald King

THROUGH blurred eyes, Steve watched the running horse. He saw him veer across the valley floor until he had reached the tall grass and his glistening body was lost in shadows. But Steve kept on watching for him. He watched until none of the gray light of early evening was left and the valley had given itself completely to the night.

Pitch had been silent, for he had seen Steve's eyes, and thought he understood. Meanwhile, he had given his attention to the Piebald, watching him move about the band, his heavy head held high and confident. The Piebald had neighed repeatedly, and the mares had slowly broken their tight ring. Once more they had begun grazing. Where only the strongest could be king, they had no choice but to accept their new leader.

At that moment, Pitch turned to Steve. But it was

as though the boy had heard nothing, had seen nothing save the red stallion. Pitch finally said, "But he wasn't killed, Steve. He was smart enough to get away."

Steve's eyes were no longer tearful, but there was still a tautness to his face. "Yes," he repeated slowly. "He was smart enough to get away. He knew he was licked." Steve's gaze met Pitch's. "How bad do you think he's been hurt?"

"Pretty bad. But if you think he ran away to die, you're worrying needlessly. He'll take care of himself all right." And when Pitch saw Steve turn to look at the burly Piebald, he added, "But they have a new leader now. They don't seem to mind it a bit, either. Just look at them, grazing away as though nothing had happened. You'd think they'd have a little to say about who's going to be their boss. But they don't, and they know it. All they can do is to accept this new king, ugly as he is."

"I'm not accepting it." Steve's voice was low and heavy with emotion.

Bewildered, Pitch turned to him. It was several seconds before he said simply, "But you've got to." Then he smiled, adding with attempted lightness, "You and I have nothing to say about this, you know, Steve."

"I've got to do something."

"But you can't, Steve!" Pitch's words were clipped. "And, frankly, I don't understand why you feel it shouldn't be this way. This is the survival of the fittest . . . a game that's been going on since the world began. Oh, I know how you feel about that red horse . . . I haven't forgotten your story of Flame. A remarkable coincidence. But you said yourself, Steve, that he knew he was licked. And it was this brute of a horse that whipped him. I don't like it either, but you've got to accept it, Steve," Pitch concluded flatly. "You couldn't possibly do anything else anyway."

"I could try to kill the Piebald." There was no doubt of the sincerity in Steve's voice.

"You're kidding," Pitch said quickly.

"No, I'm not, Pitch."

It was too dark to see Steve's eyes. Pitch said, "You're being silly, Steve. Come on . . . let's get the fire going and have some food."

But the boy didn't move, and his head was still turned toward the band . . . toward the Piebald. "If only we'd brought a gun," he said almost to himself. "I could have killed him with a gun. Still, there must be some other way."

"Steve!" Pitch's voice was shrill. "What in the world is the matter with you! You try killing that vicious horse and you'll be killed yourself! I won't have any more of this foolish talk. These horses were here long before we were born, and they'll be here long after we're dead. Why get so excited over the Piebald? He means nothing to you."

"But he does! Can't you understand, Pitch?" Steve asked, turning quickly to his friend. "Can't you see that if the Piebald is left as their leader this breed will never be the same? His blood will be in every single foal, Pitch. They'll be like him and much worse in a very few years."

After a long silence Pitch said quietly, "So that's what's troubling you. But you still can't do anything about it, Steve. You couldn't possibly do anything. If it's the end of this particular breed of horse, it's the end . . . that's all."

"But not if I can kill the Piebald," Steve insisted.

"You're not making sense, Steve," Pitch returned angrily. "And I'm not going to allow you to risk your neck trying to kill him, either. The only one who could possibly do away with the Piebald is that red horse, and I'm afraid he won't be back for another try."

"But maybe he will, Pitch!" Steve said excitedly. "Maybe that's it! Maybe he will come back!"

"Maybe he will," Pitch agreed resignedly, walking back to the cave.

Steve was behind him, his voice eager now. "Maybe that's why he ran away . . . so he can come back again, I mean! He's an intelligent animal, Pitch. Don't forget that."

"I'm not forgetting it," Pitch returned agreeably.

Steve didn't speak again until after they had opened their packs, and then his voice had lost its eagerness. "Or do you think, Pitch," he asked slowly, "that he took too much today, that he'll never be the same? I've heard of such things happening to prize fighters."

"This is a horse, Steve," Pitch replied, "not a prize fighter. And, frankly, I don't know anything about either of them."

A few minutes later the fire was licking greedily beneath their stove.

"Pitch . . ."

Pitch turned to the boy, noting the tense face, the bright, excited eyes. "What is it now, Steve?" he asked.

"Tomorrow I'm going to look for Flame. Maybe I can help him some way. Maybe I can do something that'll get him back to fight the Piebald . . . when he's well again, I mean."

"Sure, Steve. Maybe it's a good idea." Pitch felt certain that Steve wouldn't even get a glimpse of the red stallion, much less be able to do anything to send him back to fight the Piebald. But searching for Flame would take his mind off the black-and-white stallion and his ridiculous notion of finding some way to kill him. Pitch found the thought comforting. "Open a can of beans, Steve," he said. "The pot is ready."

Steve set out alone early the next morning. Reaching the valley floor, he began crossing it to get to the far side. The horses had moved down the valley, but still could be easily seen.

As Steve walked along, his gaze remained on the Piebald. The breeze was coming from upwind, carrying the boy's scent to the stallion. But Steve didn't think that he was in any danger. The stallion would fight anything that threatened his supremacy of the band, but he wouldn't go out looking for trouble. Steve realized, too, that his scent was something entirely new to the Piebald. It would bother him and he would be curious, but only if Steve approached the band would he be in any danger. And Steve planned to keep far away from the horses. He had nothing with which to protect himself. One of the coils of rope was all he carried, and that, he had told Pitch, was for Flame just in case he got close to him. Steve knew Pitch was watching him. He had promised him he'd go to the far side of the valley, away from the horses, before making his way down.

The Piebald stood at gaze, his long ears pricked forward, his large face, half black, half white, still turned in Steve's direction. For several minutes he stood there, his small eyes unwavering. Then he lowered his heavy head to the grass.

Steve's pace quickened until he was running. Reaching the tall grass, he found it to be young wild cane like that which he had seen on Antago. Flimsy as it was, he welcomed it as a protection. It grew high, almost to his chest. He crouched low beneath it and only the bending of the stalks betrayed his presence.

Cautiously he made his way to the end of the cane; then he stopped to take in his surroundings. There were some trees between him and the yellow walls. More of them grew along the edge of the cane and down the side of the valley. They would afford him some protection if he needed it. Now he slowly raised his head in the direction of the Piebald and his band, noting with relief that the Piebald was still grazing and had moved closer to the band. So far, so good. It would appear that the black-and-white stallion had decided to ignore him, since Steve did not seem to be a threat to him or his newly acquired band.

Bending down again, Steve started down the valley, taking short, fast steps. But it wasn't until he had passed opposite the place where the Piebald and his band were grazing that he breathed easily and ceased raising his head every so often above the cane to look at them.

Now Steve was downwind from the Piebald and he felt comparatively safe. His pace quickened. His destination was approximately two miles still farther down the valley. When he arrived there he would look across the valley floor for the lone tree with the red cluster of flowers that grew alongside the green-carpeted valley floor. It was a little past that tree where he had seen Flame turn into the tall cane, running in the direction of the yellow walls until he became lost in the shadows.

More than an hour had passed when Steve raised his head to find that he was just about opposite the tree across the valley that he was using as his marker. He continued walking another hundred yards or more, then entered the tall cane again, making his way to the green-carpeted floor. Reaching the edge of the cane, he peered through the stalks and saw that the band was still far up the valley. The distance between them was too great for them to notice him as he walked quickly onto the green grass. Halfway across, he broke into a run and didn't stop until he had reached the cane on the other side of the valley.

Now he was below the tree and near the spot where he had seen Flame entering the tall cane. His eyes followed the line of stalks from where he stood to the tree. There was no break in the line, no evidence of broken or bent stalks to disclose Flame's path. Steve then turned in the opposite direction, his gaze still following the edge of the cane. There was nothing there either to show that the horse had gone through. Knowing that Flame had passed the tree, Steve began walking farther down the valley. He had gone about three hundred yards when he came upon the broken stalks. Quickly he followed the path swept clear by the running horse.

10

The Chase

─────────

THE field of wild cane was no wider than a hundred yards at most, and when Steve emerged from it he found that there was a long, gradual slope to the yellow, precipitous walls. He looked around for some trace of Flame's trail, but his untrained eyes found no evidence of flying hoofs over the grassy plain.

For some time he stood there undecided, sweeping his eyes over the yellow walls, then along their base. Finally he set out, traveling down the valley toward a thin cloud of vapor beginning to rise from the ground about a mile away. Surely, he decided, there was no other direction in which Flame could have gone. The base of the walls was an unbroken line of sheer, bare rock which towered hundreds of feet into the sky. Like himself, the red stallion could have had no alternative but to go down the valley.

The ground before him began to fall gradually toward the hollow from which the mist rose. Steve stopped to rest for a moment and looked behind him at the valley, at the bending cane and beyond that at the valley floor, rich in grass and colorful foliage. Then he turned back to the desolate land ahead of him, throwing the rope he carried over his shoulder. He was near enough to the vapors to smell their foul stench. They came from a patch of marshland, as he had thought. And, as the sun began to rise above the walls to the east, the vapors thickened as though in resentment of Steve's approach.

But the sickening smells of rotting vegetation did not stop him; instead Steve's pace quickened as he approached the marsh. He felt certain that Flame had come this way, and with the ground already becoming soft and wet beneath his feet, there was the possibility of finding the stallion's hoofprints. Upon reaching the border of the dismal swamp, Steve came to a stop. To the left the vapors reached almost to the walls, and to his right they extended almost to the cane. How deep the marsh went he could not tell.

Steve kept his eyes on the ground as he walked along the edge of the marsh. He was but fifty yards from the walls when he came to an abrupt halt. Quickly he dropped to his knees, running his hands over the soft earth. He had found Flame's hoofprints and they led straight into the marsh!

He hesitated a moment and thought of waiting for

the vapors to subside. They were probably at their worst in the sun's first rays. Perhaps when Flame had entered the marsh last night there had been none at all. But why even think about that! He was on the track of the red stallion and perhaps too close to him already to delay his search any longer than was absolutely necessary. Holding his breath, Steve plunged into the gray, cloudlike world.

Within the marsh, he saw a slimy wilderness of high reeds and swamp ferns dotted with many small black pools and broken only by long, green narrow avenues of what was comparatively solid ground. It was down these strips of green that Flame's trail led. Steve followed them cautiously. The vapors weren't as dense as he had expected, but the stench, when he finally had to breathe, was almost more than he could stand. Yet he kept on, encouraged by the evidence before him that the red stallion had gone on ahead and that the vapors were thinning in the direction he was traveling.

Flame's trail zigzagged with the green strips, but Steve knew from the gradual rise of the land that he was going toward the walls. He never relaxed his vigil as he walked along slowly, treading carefully over the ground. Quagmires, heavy with sucking, all-engulfing quicksand, were on each side of him. That Flame had passed over this same route did not make Steve less cautious. And as he went farther along, he was certain that Flame knew his way very well.

There had been no hesitancy or break in the stallion's stride, for his hoofprints were regular and long enough for a slow gallop.

In a little while the vapors became mere whisps and the ground became more and more solid beneath Steve's feet. The pull upward became more abrupt and as the air cleared, becoming almost fresh again, Steve breathed deeply and walked faster.

At last he was completely free of the marsh, and he stopped abruptly, astounded at what he saw ahead of him. On either side were the high yellow cliffs and before him a long, steep channel penetrating deeply within the walls! Flame's hoofprints were no longer visible on the hard ground, but Steve had no doubt that the stallion had gone on ahead.

His heart pounding heavily, more from excitement than from the exertion of his climb, Steve followed the channel which, he decided, at one time had been the bed of a stream emptying into the marsh below. The dry stream bed was strewn with rocks and Steve picked his way slowly among them. The course, although still steep, began to twist and turn, the yellow walls closing in more and more.

For another quarter of an hour Steve walked up the gorge. He picked his way with great care for the stream bed was pitted with deep holes. Steve wondered how Flame had managed to go up this passage without breaking a leg. The red stallion had passed through here many times before, there was no doubt of that. Finally Steve came to the end of the gorge and before his eyes stretched a green sliver of a valley, not more than half a mile long and only three hundred yards or so wide. Through the center of it ran the dry stream bed, with short, green grass on either side that became lost in the wild cane which spread to the walls.

Steve stood silently in awe at his discovery of the new valley. It gleamed like a green gem placed in a setting of yellow gold. The high cliffs surrounding it enhanced its solemn beauty and breathtaking solitude.

So overwhelmed was Steve by his discovery that it was a matter of minutes before he saw the red stallion. Flame was grazing less than half the valley away from Steve, and the boy's body became rigid as he looked upon him with unbelieving eyes. The stallion walked over to a stream and stretched his long, graceful neck down to it, his red coat blazing in the sun.

When Steve finally moved it was in the direction of the cane. He walked quickly, yet his eyes never left the red stallion, who still hadn't become aware of his presence. Steve wanted to get close to him. It never occurred to him that he might be in danger from the red stallion, for this was his horse and there was no fear within him. He had known this moment before, for very often in his dreams he had approached Flame as he was doing now.

Steve had reached the tall cane and was in a crouched position when the stallion raised his head and turned it in the boy's direction.

Not a muscle of the red stallion's body moved, but he sensed danger. His coat and long mane were matted with his opponents' blood as well as his own; his mouth was raw-red from the fury of his battles. Yet he raised his head arrogantly and fire still burned in his startled eyes. He was alert and suspicious of an enemy he could not see. The scent that came to his sensitive nostrils was of an animal unknown to him. His small head moved slowly over the grass, his neck so tense that the great muscles bulged beneath his velvet-soft coat. He was accustomed to facing danger. Yet now, after a few minutes of patient watchfulness, he turned away, frightened. Quickly he moved farther up the valley. The fear that was slowly taking over his tired body was as new and strange to him as the scent that now came to his nostrils.

Steve had remained absolutely still, close enough to watch the stallion as he wheeled on rigid hind legs and made off for the far end of the valley.

Now he stood up amidst the cane, realizing that the stallion knew of his presence in the valley. He can't go far, Steve told himself, there's no place to go up there.

And there's no sense in my hiding from him, he thought. The only way I can do anything for him is to win his confidence. He's more beautiful than

anything I've ever dreamed of! If there ever was a
perfect horse, he's it. And he's not hurt badly. I can
tell from the free, easy strides he's taking. He's been
cut up some. But he'll be well in a few days, for
wounds heal fast in a wild, healthy animal like him.
He's tired more than anything else now. I know he
can beat the Piebald. He could whip anything! He
was smart enough to get away, to wait until he's
ready to meet the Piebald again, and on an equal
basis. He'll go back to his band. He's been their
leader too long to keep away from them, to live
alone . . . an outcast.

At the end of the valley, the red stallion came to a
stop, then wheeled around. His small ears were
pricked forward, alert for the slightest sound; his
muscles were tense and ready, as were his wits. But
he needed only his eyes to see his foe. His shifting
gaze easily picked up the two-legged figure walking
through the tall grass, coming steadily in his direction. His gigantic body trembled and he opened his
blood-caked mouth to bare his teeth. He moved
about restlessly, but neither drew away nor advanced
to meet this new foe. His thin-skinned nostrils
quivered, then curled. Finally he shattered the stillness of the valley with his whistle . . . shrill, loud
and clear, it reverberated from wall to wall!

Then that new feeling was there again. It probed
the ravaged body of the red stallion until it found and
engulfed his heart. Shaking his fiery head, he pawed
the ground. That new feeling had come during his

fight with the black-and-white stallion and now was part of him. His splendid body trembled, as always before an encounter with a foe. But he knew it was different this time. His trembling was not caused by tension, excitement or ruthlessness, but by a fear that now dominated every inch of him. Accepting it, he turned again, running with long, ground-covering bounds away from the figure that was tracking him.

Steve had crossed the short grass and was walking alongside the dry stream bed when he saw Flame turn and head up the grassy slope toward the base of the walls. He didn't know whether to be surprised that the stallion had run away from him. He had never tracked a wild horse before. Yet momentarily he remembered the savageness of the Piebald, born wild as Flame had been. The Piebald hadn't run away, but then he had had a band to protect; and that, Steve decided, must be the difference in their reactions to the sight of him.

If I can just get close enough to show him I don't mean any harm, Steve thought. If I can just do that.

The walls toward which Flame ran were the highest in the valley, rising almost a thousand feet, with their summits touching the sky. At their base the rock was neither sheer nor precipitous, Steve found, but pierced with narrow crags and chasms. And into one of those indentations in the walls Steve saw Flame suddenly disappear!

Walking faster, Steve went up the slope until

creeping shadows from the walls above swallowed the brightness of the late morning sun. Ahead of him was the dark tunnel from which the stream came, and a little to the left of it, the narrow chasm where Flame had gone.

The chasm led ever downward. Steve hadn't gone very far when he realized that no river had cut this passage; possibly a giant disturbance of nature, such as an earthquake, had made the cleavage through the walls. The course was straight, with no twisting or turning as in the gorge. The walls overhead were jagged and torn, so much so that at times they shut out the blue sky from Steve's wondrous gaze.

As he walked down the chasm, he felt the great gusts of wind that came intermittently at him. His pace became faster, for he knew that only an outlet to the sea could cause such a wind within the walls of the island. Where was Flame taking him? To what would this trail lead? Leaning against the wind, which was now blowing steadily, Steve broke into a half-run down the steep grade.

Finally he came to a level stretch of ground, at the end of which the chasm stopped. Ahead of Steve loomed a large, black hole. He ran to it, then came to an abrupt halt, for even above the wind he could hear the heavy thud of waves pounding upon rock.

His excitement mounting, Steve proceeded into the hole, cautiously at first until his eyes became accustomed to the semi-darkness, then faster, ever faster. As he walked along he noticed that it was becoming much lighter ahead. The tunnel was high and wide, and there was every evidence that it had been made by the sea. The walls on either side were porous and of varied colors, including pinks, greens, grays and whites. Sea moss hung from the coral rock.

Steve's heart beat rapidly as he rushed headlong around a sharp turn, the sound of crashing waves loud in his ears. Then he brought himself up suddenly. Directly ahead of him was a great cavern, about seventy-five feet in length, equally high, and fifty-odd feet wide! Through the center of it ran a narrow canal, its waters flooding and ebbing with the waves as they struck the outside walls and found their way into the cavern through a low but wide hole at the base of the walls.

Steve's startled eyes turned quickly from the sea hole back to the canal. The sides of it were lined with green moss-covered piles that poked their way through the fine white sand that covered the floor of the cavern. This, then, at one time had been the landing place for the boats from the Spanish galleons that had anchored off this island! Through the sea hole the Conquistadores were able to bring their loot and their armies within the natural fortress of Azul Island! And the chances of anyone else's finding their entrance from the sea were very slight. No enemy would have noticed it, Steve felt certain . . . any more than he and Pitch had when they had gone around the island looking for a place to scale the walls.

For several minutes Steve stood there, transfixed. Then he suddenly became filled with concern. Where was Flame? Surely he had to be here . . . this definitely was the end of the chase! Steve's gaze left the canal and traveled over the walls of the cavern.

The cavern was bathed in the soft glow of a peculiarly colored light brought about, perhaps, by the varied colors in the rock. Slowly Steve walked into the cavern and found that for some reason he was uneasy, even a little frightened. Why he should be, he didn't know. But the feeling was there and he couldn't fight it down. He had gone only a few yards when he came upon an adjoining cave to his right. Startled, he drew back, for he had not been able to see it from where he had stood before.

The cave was small and the light gray and dim inside. But Steve had no trouble seeing the large wooden structure that dominated it. A large heavy pole rose fifteen or more feet above the ground, and from the top extended a wooden arm from which hung a long, heavy chain reaching halfway to the ground. As Steve continued to look at the structure, he noticed other details. He saw the iron band, dangling from the end of the chain . . . a band like the one he had seen when he and Pitch had come upon the chamber of the dead! And he realized that the chain was used to support a suspended weight and that the structure itself was a derrick crane. He saw the tackle running along across the wooden arm, then down the large supporting pole until it came to what looked like a metal wheel with a handle for turning. Cautiously Steve moved toward the structure.

He was only a few yards away when he made out the black pool beneath the hanging chain. He reached the edge of it by going carefully down a rather steep grade which encircled the pool. The water was but a few inches beneath the rim and he saw that it just covered a brownish mud or sand. Immediately Steve remembered the quagmires back in the marsh and he felt sure it was a quicksand pit. Seeing a large piece of timber lying on the ground near by, he picked it up and shoved it into the pool. Slowly the pole disappeared into the quicksand until it was completely covered over.

Steve turned away and didn't stop until he had reached the level floor of the chamber. Nervously he removed his rope and transferred it from one shoulder to the other. He'd had enough of this place. He wanted to leave. But first he had to make sure Flame wasn't in this cave. His gaze shifted about until it reached the depths of the chamber. The light was a gray-black there, and he would have to go forward to make certain Flame wasn't there.

Steve passed the crane, walking cautiously and

very much afraid. He was almost at the farthest end now. A few more strides and he would turn back to the lighter cavern beyond. Perhaps he had spent too much time here. Perhaps Flame already had gone back through the chasm.

He was about to turn when he saw a slight movement against the rocks. Startled and frightened, he drew back. He didn't know what it was, but he didn't think of it as being Flame. He was too scared for that. He backed away quickly, stumbling and falling to one knee. Then came a sudden movement from the blacker-than-black form in front of him. He turned and ran, cutting across the chamber. And it was then that he heard the heavy thud of hoofs upon sand, saw the gigantic shape of the red stallion coming from his right! Steve turned again, as frightened as the stallion, who veered sharply away from him.

Steve saw Flame and the crane at the same time, and tried to avoid them both by flinging himself to the sandy floor. Then came a wild, horrible scream from the stallion as his hind legs caught in the rim of the short, steep embankment descending to the pit. Thrown off balance by the abrupt grade, Flame pummeled the earth with his forelegs in an attempt to regain his balance. But his hind weight carried him over the rim, and before Steve's frantic eyes the red stallion slid into the pool of sucking death!

11

Sucking Death

———

For a few minutes all fear left the red stallion and fighting fury took its place. His hindquarters were in the pit, but he still held on to the rim with his pounding forelegs. He was fighting the battle of his life *for* his life, and his body swelled with untamed fierceness.

But the pit was an enemy far more formidable than the burly Piebald, more deadly than any living creature. And as the red stallion beat the earth with his forelegs, the pit slowly, steadily pulled his hindquarters deeper and deeper into its soft, yielding bosom.

Steve had remained by the crane but had risen to his knees. His body was limp, his senses numb, and only his eyes seemed at all alive as he watched the scene before him. Flame's fight for his life was unreal and the fury of it didn't wholly penetrate the boy's

138

dazed mind for a few seconds. But when it did, and he became aware of the sinking hindquarters, the terrible, pounding forelegs of the stallion, fear passed from him to be replaced by a frenzy such as he'd never felt before.

Steve moved quickly, wildly about the pit, not knowing what to do for the horse and wasting valuable time. It wasn't until he slipped on the steep grade descending to the rim of the pit and brought himself to a stop by falling to the ground and digging his heels and hands into the loose dirt that his own narrow escape from the pit drove the frenzy out of his mind and he was able to think clearly.

Sitting on the ground, his heels still braced in the dirt, he looked at the raging horse. If only he would stop fighting so hard! If only he would keep his body still and his forelegs rigid on the rim, he wouldn't sink so fast!

Steve was filled with anxiety for the stallion; he had an overpowering desire to help. But what could he do? Where would he start? There was that chain hanging over the pit. . . . A minute later Steve moved toward the crane's supporting pole with a swiftness that only comes in moments of great stress, when actions are never remembered in detail.

Reaching the pole with long, quick strides, he bent down, picking up the rope that he had dropped during his fall. Then he returned to the pit, moving closer to the stallion than he'd been before.

The horse's forefeet had stopped thrashing and now moved only when his hoofs slipped on the loose dirt of the pit's rim. His arrogant head, with teeth bared, was turned toward the boy, but Steve was unmindful of it. His attention was fixed on Flame's hindquarters. Momentarily the stallion had stopped sinking. If he continued to remain still there might be time to save him.

The boy studied the chain dangling a few feet above and a little to the rear of the stallion. He had to get his rope through the iron band at the end. For a matter of seconds there was indecision in Steve's eyes; then quickly he made his way to the supporting pole, stopping for a second to gaze at the metal wheel around which the chain was wound. Steve's hand went toward the handle of the wheel but he did not touch it. There would be time for that later, he told himself. He heard Flame resume pounding his hoofs and knew he had to work even faster. The coil of rope went about his neck and his arms reached high up the supporting pole and around it. Then he jumped, clearing the wheel, and his legs encircled the pole. His arms reached higher on the pole, and his shoulder muscles bulged through his thin shirt as he pulled himself up, his legs wrapped securely about the pole.

Upon reaching the top, Steve looked across at the wooden arm extending over the pit. He pressed his hand down on it, and found it solid and steady. Gradually he placed all his weight upon it until he was convinced that the aged wood was as strong as it had ever been.

He moved across the arm, straddling it with his legs locked together beneath him and with his hands moving along in front. Only once did he look down at the stallion and pit fifteen feet below; he saw that Flame's haunches had sunk deeper into the quicksand with the stallion's renewed, futile efforts to escape. Steve's movements became faster until he was within reaching distance of the hanging chain.

Drawing the heavy chain to him until he had hold of the iron band at its end, he removed the rope about his neck and doubled it, drawing the two ends through the band and tying them securely to it. He now had a long noose hanging from the end of the chain. Slowly he lowered the chain, then flung the rope down to the rim of the pit. That done, he made his way back quickly along the arm and shinnied down the pole.

Upon reaching the ground, he ran to where he'd thrown his rope. He picked it up and went toward the stallion, his strides slower now and more cautious. Taking hold of the doubled rope, he separated the two parts, forming a noose. Then he turned to the stallion, knowing that the most difficult job of all was ahead. For now he had to get the noose about Flame's girth!

Carrying the rope, Steve approached the red

stallion. For the first time he was able to get a good look at the red-raw mouth now speckled with white foam, the matted blood upon the long mane. The stallion shifted his eyes toward him, and there was a brightness, a savageness to them that sent cold tremors through the boy's body.

The red stallion's forefeet slipped closer to the edge of the pit and his furious pounding began again. But powerful though his legs were, they could not free him from the deadly quicksand that had pulled its prey down as far as the flanks.

Steve twisted the doubled rope nervously, parted the two pieces again, then pulled the rope as taut as he could, swinging the chain far over the plunging stallion. Now for the hardest part of the job!

He took a step toward the stallion, knowing he would have no more than a foot of clearance between himself and Flame's head when he tried to get the lower part of the noose under the horse. And as Steve neared the stallion, the noose stretched wide, he began talking to Flame in a soft voice, not betraying his fear.

"You're my horse, Flame. I've known you for a long time . . . and you've known me. When I first saw you, you were standing on the cliff. But it wasn't just a couple of days ago . . . it was many years ago. And when you first came to me and I followed you, very much as I did today, you fought me . . . just as you're doing now. And you were afraid of me then. You thought I meant to harm you, but I didn't at all. And you found that out, just as you'll learn it now, Flame. I want . . ."

Steve was getting very close to the red stallion, whose teeth were still bared and who was still snorting with rage and pain. For only a second did the boy stop talking, but there was no hesitancy to his slow-moving footsteps. He knew he couldn't come to a halt now because if he did the red stallion would know of his fear and it would be the end. He must continue walking forward, as though he belonged with the stallion. It was that or forever lose his horse.

"Keep walking. Keep talking," he told himself aloud. "It doesn't matter what I say, it's only the sound of my voice that matters to him. But don't stop. Keep talking and keep going toward him. Isn't that right, Flame? You know me. You know my voice. You've heard it before. I've heard yours before, too. Your scream rises to such a high pitch that it sounds like a whistle that no other whistle can match. But you're in a mess now. That's what I meant when I said I wanted to help you. You're in a spot where you can't get out by yourself. You need help, Flame. You need me. Just . . ."

Steve was close enough now to the stallion to have the white foam splatter upon him. Close enough to begin feeling the stallion's hot breath upon his outstretched hands as they held the rope.

The red stallion flung his hoofs at Steve but

143

stopped when he found himself slipping farther back toward the pit. His forelegs became still and rigid again, but his glaring eyes never left the boy.

Steve went on talking, but now he shifted his gaze to the lower part of the noose that hung to one side of Flame. Raising his left hand, he held the upper part of the noose above the stallion's head. It was time to pass in front of the horse now. The stretch of rope gave him less than a foot of leeway. His body and raised hand would be clear of the raking teeth, but his other hand, carrying the lower part of the noose, would be within striking range of the stallion's hoofs.

There was a wavering to Steve's low voice as he moved in front of the stallion, but recognizing it as fear, he drove it from him and his voice became steady again. "You've got to help me now, Flame. The rope's got to go under your forelegs. It means you'll have to raise them again. Just once more, then you can keep them still again."

Haunches deep in the wet mud that held him fast, the red stallion swelled to greater fury at the nearness of this foe, who had tracked him down. He sensed the sucking death behind him, yet his forelegs still trod upon solid ground and his untamed heart would not admit defeat. But now this new enemy approached him, when he was unable to fight back! He bared his teeth, waiting. And all the time he heard the soft sounds this foe uttered as he approached him. He had never heard such sounds before, nor seen a

144

foe who walked on hind legs only. His eyes met the newcomer's. Shaking his head, the stallion snorted repeatedly in rage and fear. Now his foe was directly in front of him. He saw the long, thin object close to his forefeet. It looked and moved like a snake. Furiously he struck at the thing and it passed quickly under his legs. Another frantic plunge at it, and it swept clear of him and entwined itself about his belly! The two-legged foe had moved away, too far for him to reach with teeth or hoofs. He screamed and pounded upon the ground in front of him, and then he felt the weight of the wet mud pulling more heavily on his hindquarters.

Carrying the lower part of the noose, Steve hurried around the rim of the pit, his heart beating wildly. He had the noose about Flame! He pulled the rope as far back to the sinking hindquarters as possible, then dropped it and ran over to the crane. Reaching the wheel, he took hold of the handle and breathed a short prayer before turning it. The handle moved, turning the wheel and winding the chain about it.

The chamber resounded to the long-unheard noise of the iron chain passing through the crane's tackle and moving down the supporting pole to the wheel. Anxiously Steve watched the end of the chain ascend until the rope became taut about the stallion's body. He knew the chain would not slip back, for the wheel was fitted with teeth into which a metal hook from the handle slipped as he turned, thus locking it

Steve had the noose around Flame

and preventing the wheel from turning in reverse unless the metal hook was released.

Now that the slack had been taken up, it was harder to turn the wheel. Steve bore down on it with all his strength, knowing that with each click of the wheel's teeth Flame's hindquarters were being lifted from the quicksand. He stopped to rest only when he saw that Flame's flanks were clear. And then he realized that he would need Pitch's help to raise Flame all the way out of the quicksand and swing him clear of the pit. After making certain the wheel was locked, Steve went over to the red stallion.

"You're safe now, Flame," he said. "You won't sink any deeper. And I'll be back soon. Then you'll be free again to go back to your band."

With one last look at his horse, Steve left the chamber at a half-run. And as he made his way back through the outer cavern and up the tunnel leading to the chasm, he was unmindful of the tiredness in his legs and the long trek back to camp.

12

Steve Makes a Promise

S TEVE slowed down a little as he went through
the chasm and then the smaller valley where he
had first seen Flame that morning, hurrying
again when he made his way to the gorge that would
take him to Blue Valley and Pitch.

After leaving the cavern and Flame, Steve had
moved as one in a stupor, his eyes unseeing and
glazed, his senses numbed; yet even so his feet had
held to the trail as though they had always known it.
The lack of expression on his face and the limpness of
his muscles were those of a person who had passed
through a great crisis without realizing exactly what
the crisis had been or the outcome.

But slowly, as he went along, the knowledge
penetrated his dazed mind that somehow he had saved
Flame from certain death. He knew that he had
placed a noose about Flame's girth . . . a noose he

had made with his rope. He knew that the noose was attached to the end of the chain that hung from the crane over the pit. He remembered that he was going back to camp to get Pitch's help in swinging Flame clear of the pit. But other than that he remembered little. The details of what he had done from the time of his fall in the cavern until he had stood before Flame, knowing that the stallion was safe from the danger of sinking deeper into the quicksand, weren't clear in his mind.

He glanced up at the sun as he entered the gorge. From its height he decided that it was early afternoon. But was it the same day? Had it been only this morning that he had set out looking for Flame? Surely it was much longer ago than that!

Steve followed the twisting, turning, dry stream bed and passed the yellow overhanging cliffs. Gradually his eyes began to lose their glazed look.

"Yes," he finally admitted aloud, "it has to be the same day. Just as it was only two days ago that I first set foot on Azul Island."

Only two days ago . . . then this was his third day here. It was incomprehensible to Steve. Surely hours and days were no way of measuring time! Time should be reckoned by events that happen to a person, and not by the lapse of hours! It seemed months ago . . . almost years . . . since he and Pitch had headed for the sandy spit of land that was known as the only habitable part of Azul Island.

149

When Steve came to the marsh, he saw that the vapors were rising only from the low end of the hollow, near the cane. He made his way down the long stretches of soft green ground which still bore Flame's hoofprints. Now for the top of the rise leading from the hollow. From there he would be able to see the floor of the valley . . . and he would be looking for the Piebald. It would be the black-and-white-streaked stallion who would dictate the direction he would take in his journey back to camp.

He was eager to reach Pitch. He would tell him how he had found Flame and helped him, just as he'd said he was going to do. He'd tell Pitch he needed his help now; it would mean going back to the cavern this very same day and probably spending the night there. Surely Pitch would understand that Flame had to be swung clear of the pit today so he could eat and recover more readily from his injuries.

I'll help Flame, Steve told himself. I'll take care of his wounds.

It had been only a short time ago that Steve had recoiled in fear at the viciousness of the stallion, yet now there was no fear within him as he thought of aiding Flame. Along with many details, his fear also was forgotten.

Reaching the flat top of the hollow, he stood looking at the grassy plain stretching before him. A little to his left was the cane, and beyond that the green velvet floor of the valley. Far off, a silken sheet of water fell from the high tunnel to the pool below.

It was a few minutes before Steve saw the Piebald and his newly-acquired band, for they had moved away from the pool and were grazing far across the valley. The boy quickened his pace when he realized that it would be safe for him to stay on his side of the valley.

When he came to the cane he bent low beneath it to keep out of sight. The Piebald was upwind from him, so Steve knew his scent would not betray his presence. All he had to do was to keep from being seen. The Piebald was too far away to give him any trouble.

As Steve drew parallel with the band, he stopped for a moment to look over the cane at the black-and-white stallion.

Heavy-bodied, the Piebald grazed alone, only occasionally turning his heavy head to the band. His white tail whisked the flies away from his streaked body and he stomped the earth with his hind legs to rid himself of the flies that avoided his long tail. His short, thick neck bulged with muscle as he stretched his head to the ground. Suddenly he stopped grazing, bringing his head up with a start. He stood motionless for a while, grass protruding from his mouth, his jaws locked. Finally he turned his head to Steve's side of the valley and watched intently; then he turned his head still farther, looking down the valley. Again he stood still, and only his small, beady eyes moved. After a long while he began chewing on the grass in his mouth, and when that was swallowed forgot his inquisitiveness and began grazing again.

Steve had bent low beneath the cane, and proceeded up the valley only when the Piebald went back to his grazing.

"It'll be different next time," Steve muttered to himself. Already he was thinking of the coming fight between Flame and the Piebald. "You won't have his band much longer," he went on, as though talking to the Piebald. "He'll come back as fresh as you were in the first fight. He belongs with his band. He was meant to be their leader."

And as he approached the waterfall, Steve's spirits rose. Soon he would be with Pitch and together they would help Flame return to his band. With Flame as its leader again, this perfect breed of horse would go on. Just now, it was what Steve wanted more than anything else in the world.

When he was almost opposite the pool he straightened, running through the cane toward the trail that would take him to the cliff above and to Pitch.

"Pitch! Pitch!" Steve began calling at the bottom of the rocky trail, his face turned upward to the looming black hole that was their camp. His tired legs carried him up the trail with a speed that was generated by his eagerness to reach Pitch. But there was no reply to his frequent shouts, no sight of his friend's thin, frail body.

But he's got to be here, Steve thought desperately. At least, he can't be far away.

When Steve reached the cave he came to a stop. On the floor were Pitch's pack and rope. Beside them stood the stove and several empty cans, evidence that Pitch had recently eaten. Steve turned to the blackness of the cave's interior. Surely Pitch wasn't in there or there would be a light. Then where was he?

Steve had walked out upon the wide ledge in front of the cave when he heard a shout from above. *Pitch!* Whirling, Steve peered up at the yellow walls rising above him.

"Yo!" Pitch called again. "Over here!"

Steve shifted his gaze to the right, from where the stream flowed out of the walls above the tunnel. And there stood Pitch, flat against what seemed to Steve to be a sheer, bare sheet of stone! He wanted to yell, but was afraid that anything he did might upset Pitch's balance. So he remained still and silent while he watched Pitch move slowly across the wall like a human fly.

A few minutes later Pitch had reached the tunnel and was coming down the trail to the cave.

"Steve!" Pitch shouted when he was still fifty yards away. "What I've found! What treasures! And it's only the beginning!"

And then Pitch had reached the ledge, the pockets

of his jacket bulging, and his eyes met Steve's. Pitch saw the concern on his friend's taut face, and his own became puzzled before breaking into a wry smile.

"You thought I was a goner up there, didn't you?" he asked. "Well, it's easier than it looks from here, Steve. There's a wide ledge . . . the side of it must have been built up by the Spaniards . . . so it's as easy as walking down a flight of stairs. There are some small caves up there, Steve, and you should see . . ."

Pitch, whose hands had gone to his pockets, broke off abruptly, puzzled again by the expression on Steve's face.

"You didn't run into any trouble, did you?" he asked with concern. "I saw that Piebald devil moving around when you first set out this morning. I was worried until you got clear across the valley and he went back to his grazing."

Suddenly a swift look of guilt swept over Pitch's face as he studied Steve's unwavering gaze. Here he was shooting off his mouth about himself, and the boy was hungry and looking very worn.

"You'd better eat," he said quickly. "And you must be dead tired. Where have you been, anyway? What have you been up to?" Pitch sheepishly withdrew empty hands from his pockets and walked toward the stove. "I'll get the fire going," he said, then added with his back turned to Steve, "I don't

154

suppose you found that red stallion. Didn't see him, did you?" Without waiting for Steve's reply, he asked, "Do you want just beans or shall I open a can of soup, too?"

"I'm not hungry," Steve said quietly. Somehow all his enthusiasm to tell Pitch everything that had happened was gone. He felt let down. Maybe he was tired . . . but he couldn't afford to be tired now. He had to get back to Flame. Desperately Steve tried to regain his lost enthusiasm. "Pitch . . ." he began.

"But you have to be hungry," Pitch interrupted. "You haven't eaten, and it's away past noon . . ."

"I know, Pitch. I know I should be hungry, but I'm not. Pitch . . ."

"You tell me while I'm getting something to eat for you . . . all right?"

"All right." But Steve didn't go on.

After a few moments of silence, Pitch spoke while he was opening a can of soup. "You found him, didn't you." It was put not as a question but stated as a fact, as though Pitch already knew what Steve's reply would be.

"Yes, I found him." For reasons Steve could not explain he now wanted Pitch to wait, to ask him about his search for Flame, rather than to tell it all as he had so eagerly planned. His eyes were drawn to Pitch's pockets again.

Was that it? he asked himself. Was it the "treasures" that Pitch valued so highly? Were they responsible for his own reluctance to tell Pitch all? Was it because he felt that Pitch thought more of the things he was carrying in his pockets than he did of the horses which were truly treasures in their own right? But even if Pitch did feel that way, Steve argued with himself, was there anything wrong in it? Pitch was a scholar, and if he preferred relics to horses, that was his business. There were plenty of people in the world who didn't love horses, or who loved other things more. Still . . .

"Did you just see him? Or get close to him? Or what?" Pitch asked with genuine interest in his voice. He placed the soup on the stove and turned around, facing Steve.

"I got close to him, Pitch. Real close. So close I guess I must have touched him. I'm not quite sure, though." Now it came easier as Steve saw the interest mounting in Pitch's eyes and the incredulous look upon his face. He felt his own enthusiasm mounting once more and he wanted to confide in Pitch. "I first saw him in the valley," he continued quickly. "He was drinking from the stream and, oh Pitch! if only you could have seen him!"

"It's funny I didn't see him," Pitch said. "Wait a minute . . . there isn't any stream running through this valley. There's no outlet to that pool below."

"It wasn't this valley, Pitch. It's another

one . . . a smaller one on the other side of the marsh."

"Marsh? What marsh? Where's a marsh and where's a smaller valley?"

Quickly Steve pointed far down to the left side of the valley. "You can just make out the hollow from here, Pitch," he said. "See the slight gray mist rising from the ground?"

"Yes, I see it all right. This morning there was more of it. I was wondering about the land there. And the valley?"

"It's after you go through the gorge to the left of the hollow. You can't see the gorge from here, but it goes right into the walls."

"What kind of gorge?"

Steve was impatient to get to his story of Flame, and managed to tell it only by replying brusquely to Pitch's frequent questions. Pitch gave him his soup and made him eat it while the beans were being heated. Then, as Steve told Pitch of his chase through the chasm and tunnel into the cavern, Pitch's queries stopped altogether.

Steve's soup cooled as he told Pitch about coming upon Flame in the smaller chamber. He had to omit details he himself couldn't remember, and Pitch did not question him, for he knew the boy would have told him had he been able to do so. It was enough, Pitch thought, that Steve hadn't been killed!

"But Flame's safe now," Steve concluded, his eyes bright and steady. "He won't sink any deeper until we get there. And we can get him out, Pitch . . ."

"What good would it do, Steve?" Pitch asked quietly after a long silence. "Why should you take any more chances? I don't think we should go any further with this business."

"Pitch! You don't mean what you're saying, do you? You can't mean it!" Steve's eyes mirrored the intensity he was feeling.

Pitch bent over the fire. He didn't like what he saw in Steve's eyes, but he felt that he was responsible for it. He was the one who had suggested they come to this island! He was the one who had kindled the boy's enthusiasm with tales of Spanish conquest. Yes, and they had found more than they had bargained for . . . much more! For here was a lost world untouched by man for centuries! A lost world with treasures for which many men would give their lives. And he and Steve had found it. But what price must they pay for their discovery? Already they had lived a lifetime in their few hours of groping about the death-black tunnels. They had survived to find this valley, but now Steve had undergone another terrible experience. How much could the boy take? He was no longer the same Steve who had set out for this island. He was no longer a boy but a man . . . very much of a man. Without turning around, Pitch listened to part of what Steve was saying.

"Can't you understand, Pitch?" Steve asked. "We can't leave him there to die! It's worse than if I'd done nothing and he'd been pulled down by the quicksand, because he'd be gone by now. You can't let him die a living death over that pit, Pitch! *I* can't! I'll have to go back alone if you won't come. And if I can't get him up by myself, I'll drop the chain."

He stopped, but Pitch still hadn't turned around to face him. Striding over to Pitch, he knelt down beside him. "Pitch, you remember what we both thought of the Conquistadores when we saw those chains about the bones of the skeletons in the dungeon." Steve's voice was husky but no longer pleading. "It's the same thing, Pitch. If I don't go back, I'll be no better than they were. He's just as much alive as any human being. I've got to go back. You see that, don't you, Pitch? I've either got to get him out or let him down all the way. You understand that, don't you?"

Steve said no more, and there was a long silence between the two.

Then Pitch said slowly and in a voice that shook with emotion, "I realize. I understand, Steve." Removing the beans from the stove, he dumped them with trembling hands into the tin plate before Steve. "Eat this, then, and we'll be going."

The tautness of Steve's muscles was released with the speed of a spring as he cried, "You mean it, Pitch! You'll go with me!"

Pitch was busy extinguishing the fire, and there was a pause before he replied, "Yes, I'm going, Steve. What else can I do?"

Steve's face sobered, then lighted up again as he began making plans for their return trip. "I want to be sure to take along the first-aid kit," he said quickly.

"Eat your food while it's hot," Pitch ordered.

Between mouthfuls Steve said, "He's been badly cut, Pitch, but I can help him. We should get back soon, though. He's probably still fighting, trying to get clear of the pit. Each hour he's there means a day longer in his recovery."

Pitch waited until Steve had finished eating before he said, "Steve, if we do succeed in getting him out of the pit, you've got to promise me that you'll have nothing more to do with him. By that I mean I want you to forget about helping him, forget about that red stallion."

"You mean . . ." Steve began.

"Exactly that, Steve," Pitch interrupted, and his voice was harsh. "You will have nothing more to do with him. It has to be that way. I know he's everything you ever hoped to see in a horse . . . and I know now, if I never quite knew before, how much you love them. But Steve, he's as vicious and wild

160

as . . . why, that Piebald! There's no difference in
their natures. They're both from the same mold.
They were born wild, Steve, and meant to stay wild.
You've got to realize that before you're killed."

"But, Pitch, Flame is different. He's not at all like
the Piebald. He *knows* me, Pitch. He knows that I
don't mean any harm to him, that I'm only trying to
help him."

"You've got to stay away from him, Steve," Pitch
said with finality. "Whether he goes back to his band
or not will be no concern of yours or mine. If we get
him out of this, you'll have to let him go where he
pleases without having anything to do with it. Only
on that understanding will I go along with you."
Pitch paused before adding, "We'll have enough to
do trying to find our way out of here. I have some
torches that'll help us in getting around the tunnels."
Then, changing the subject abruptly, "Picked up
another spur and a pistol today," and he tapped his
pockets.

But Steve wasn't listening. After several minutes
he said quietly, "Do you mean what you said, Pitch?
That if we get him out, *I have to let him go where he
pleases* . . ."

"Exactly," Pitch replied, ". . . without chasing
him any more or trying to help that wild stallion,
who doesn't want any help."

"Okay, Pitch," Steve said thoughtfully. "I agree.
I'll let him go where he pleases." But there was a

brightness to his eyes that Pitch didn't understand.

"You take a rest now, while I clean the pots," Pitch said. "You need a rest."

Steve stretched out upon the ground, his head on his pack. "We'd better take our packs," he said, closing his eyes, "just in case we have to spend the night there."

"Sure," Pitch replied.

"And Pitch, wait'll you see him close! You'll forget all about those things in your pockets. You've never in your life . . ." Steve's voice dropped to a mumble, then died altogether as he dozed off.

Pitch's gaze left Steve for the pot he held in his hand. "I can hardly wait," he muttered, ". . . hardly."

13

Lowered Head

━━━━━━

THE western walls of the valley were casting lengthening shadows over the cane as Steve and Pitch, crouched low, cautiously moved along beside it.

"You shouldn't have let me fall asleep," Steve said.

"You needed it," Pitch replied bluntly. "And we have hours of daylight ahead of us." He pulled his pack higher on his back, but his eyes never left the bent-over figure ahead of him. After a while he asked with concern, "You don't think that Piebald has moved, do you, Steve? Maybe we'd better look again."

"We just got through looking," Steve replied. "It's better for us to keep going until we get downwind from him."

"Maybe he's coming across for water," Pitch insisted gravely. "I don't like this business, you

163

know. That Piebald is capable of doing almost anything."

"He can't see us," Steve said. "Just a few hundred yards more, Pitch . . . then we'll look again. We should be well downwind from him by then."

Pitch grunted in response, and Steve hurried forward faster than ever. His thoughts turned from the Piebald to Flame. He still had to figure out how to swing the stallion clear of the pit. He had thought of a few ways but had discarded them. Suddenly he said, "You've got your rope, haven't you, Pitch?"

"Yeah," Pitch replied shortly; then after a pause, "You're sure we ought to go through with this, Steve? I don't like being down here. What if the Piebald turns on us? Let him be their leader. Why risk our lives to save that red stallion? I really don't see what difference it makes who leads this band. And I don't understand what you mean when you say that it does."

Steve didn't answer and they walked on until the hollow was but a quarter of a mile below them.

"We'll look for the Piebald now," Steve said, "and then beat it for the marsh." When he turned around, Pitch's head was already above the cane.

"They've moved more to the center of the valley," Pitch whispered excitedly, ducking his head again and turning to the boy. "And there's a couple of them not more than a hundred yards away!"

Steve, raising his head slowly above the cane, saw

that the Piebald and his band had moved a little closer
to them, as Pitch had said. But the black-and-white
stallion was still grazing and didn't appear to be
suspicious of anything. The two horses which had
moved away from the band and were grazing near by
were a bay mare and her stilt-legged foal. Steve felt
that the chances of the Piebald's coming over were
slim unless the mare squealed.

Steve knew that he should hide below the cane
again, but momentarily his eyes rested upon the foal,
watching the young colt as he vigorously encircled
his mother, seeking her long black tail and shaking
mane for protection against the flies that bothered
him. He couldn't be more than a couple of weeks old,
Steve figured. Noting the colt's perfect wedge-
shaped head, he thought of Flame. Surely this foal
had been sired by the red stallion. There were many
like him in the band.

"What are you doing?" Pitch asked nervously.
"See anything? Let's get going, if we're going on!"
His head too had risen above the cane beside Steve's.

Together they watched the colt, who had stopped
encircling the mare and now was stretching his head
toward the grass. His legs were too long and his neck
too short for him to reach it, so cautiously he bent his
forelegs until he was kneeling down. He pulled at the
grass, not liking it at all; then he struggled to his long
legs again and once more began encircling the mare.

Pitch and Steve were on their way again, and after

several minutes Steve said thoughtfully, "That colt was *him*, Pitch. That's exactly what I meant."

"I don't get you."

"I mean that's the sort of foal Flame sires. They're beautiful . . . everything that he is."

"Sure."

"It would be much different if the Piebald had sired those foals."

"Sure," Pitch repeated.

"I mean it, Pitch."

"I know you mean it."

"Every bad trait in the Piebald would show up in his foals," Steve continued earnestly. "They'd be monstrosities . . . all of them."

Pitch was silent a while and then he said, "And if Flame does come back to his band, some day he'll be dethroned and possibly killed by one of his own sons. Have you thought of that?"

"Yes," Steve said slowly. "I've thought of that. There can only be one stallion in the band who'll be the leader."

"Some of those colts must be almost a year old now," Pitch went on. "It won't be long before things come to a head . . . less than a couple of years, perhaps." Pitch paused, before saying suggestively, "That ought to make you realize how little difference it actually makes who's king of this band . . . Flame or the Piebald. Either one of them will eventually be killed by a younger and stronger stallion."

There was a weary note in Steve's voice as he said, "But it may take a very long time before one of these colts is able to defeat Flame or the Piebald. In that time the Piebald, if he remains the band's leader, can sire many foals, and this breed will never be the same as it is now. Yes, Pitch, it does make a difference . . . a great deal of difference."

They went on to the marsh in silence, and it was only when Steve set out over the green paths that Pitch spoke again. "You're certain this ground will hold us?" he asked.

Steve pointed to Flame's hoofprints in the soft earth, as though they were all the explanation necessary, and kept going. He was anxious to get back to the cavern, for it was hours since he had left Flame and he was very conscious of the struggle his horse must be having. He had decided, too, how he and Pitch would attempt to swing Flame clear of the pit.

When they reached the dry stream bed, they followed it into the gorge. Pitch's exclamations rose with the ascent, but ceased altogether when they reached the smaller valley. Steve too was moved again, even more deeply this time, by the solemn splendor of the hidden valley.

As they started across the valley floor there was no need for him to urge Pitch to greater speed.

Steve called a halt when they reached the spot where the stream had been diverted across the valley. "Let's leave our packs here, Pitch," he said. "There's no need to carry them the rest of the way. And if we make camp tonight, don't you think it should be here? Where we can get water, I mean."

"Yes. Yes," Pitch returned quickly, anxious to be on his way. He had his pack off before Steve and was already walking toward the chasm when Steve called to him.

"Your rope, Pitch. Where is it? We'll need it."

"It's in my pack," Pitch replied without stopping.

Steve got the rope and ran after Pitch, managing to catch up to him only when he had reached the entrance to the chasm.

Pitch took in the jagged walls rising above them. Then he turned to Steve, and his voice wavered as he said, "You realize what we're doing, don't you, Steve? We're following the footsteps of the Conquistadores. This was their way to and from Blue Valley. And we're the first, the very first ones . . ." Without finishing the sentence Pitch walked forward again, and Steve followed.

The gusts of wind coming from the tunnel beyond began blowing in their faces as they made their way down the chasm; eventually they heard the sound of crashing waves on the outer walls.

There was no time for talk now, and they went forward eagerly, one thinking of his horse, the other of the Conquistadores' exit to the sea.

When they reached the tunnel, Pitch, who still led, slowed his pace until the light became brighter as they went along; then he hurried on. But he came to an abrupt halt as the tunnel opened into the large cavern and before them, in the room's vari-colored light, was the canal leading to the sea.

Pitch stood there for a long while, and Steve was about to pass him when he moved quickly toward the canal. Steve followed, stopping again as he came to the adjoining chamber which Pitch had passed in his haste. Turning, Steve went inside.

When Pitch reached the canal, he saw the sunken, moss-covered piles. His hands touched them almost caressingly as he thought of the long centuries they had been there; then he gazed intently at the colorful coral rock. He moved forward, watching the water in the canal rise and fall with the sea swells that came from the outer world. Upon reaching the hole, he stood to one side of it where he could see a little of the ocean. The wind tore through the hole, whipping the spray upon him until his face was wet.

"Steve," he said quietly, "there must be a channel outside, running right up to this entrance. The way must be clear through the reef and rocks, because they must have brought their boats in here. This hole is higher than I thought it would be from your description, but there must be some plant life on the outside that keeps it from being seen . . . that and the waves would hide it unless one got really close. The Spaniards must have protected this entrance with guns in the walls above and on the sides. I believe we could find them if we looked, Steve. . . ."

Pitch turned, expecting to find the boy close behind him.

"Steve!" he called excitedly. "Steve! Where are you?" But his voice was lost in the roar of wind and waves.

Pitch went running back through the cavern until he saw the adjoining chamber. He stopped in front of it, startled by the semi-darkness within; then, when his eyes became accustomed to the dim light, he went inside.

Pitch walked forward a few yards, his eyes wide with amazement at the sight before him. He caught only a glimpse of the heavy wooden structure he knew was the crane, for his gaze left it immediately for the sunken rim of the pit upon which Steve was kneeling beside the still form of what had to be the red stallion.

Pitch's pace slowed until he came to a halt a short distance behind Steve and Flame.

But it can't be the same horse, he thought. It can't be!

There was nothing beautiful or proud or defiant about this horse, whose limp body hung heavily upon the rope noose that extended from the end of the chain and encircled the hind part of his body. Only one foreleg remained upon the rim of the pit and that was still; the other hung below him, dangling above the quicksand. White lather covered his body, from the flanks that rose above the quicksand to the small lowered head.

This can't be the same horse, Pitch thought again. It couldn't be the tall, long-limbed stallion who so proudly and gallantly had defended his band! This could be any horse outside Blue Valley . . . and he looks beaten, exhausted, almost dead.

Then Pitch became aware of soft murmurings within the chamber. Startled, he whirled around, his eyes seeking the chamber's dark corners. Above the heavy sounds coming from the outer cavern, he still could hear the other, softer sounds. He moved closer to Steve, and as he did, the murmurings became more distinct, finally resolving into Steve's voice! But there was a soft, melodious quality to it that Pitch had never heard in Steve's voice before. And for some unexplainable reason, Pitch found himself thinking of the look that had come into Steve's eyes that day. They went together, somehow . . . the eyes and the voice.

Pitch remained still, listening to Steve; not so much to what the boy said as to the sound of his voice.

"It's done now, Flame," Steve was saying. "It's over. You don't have to fight any more. We're going to get you out now. You'll be free again."

When Steve had first arrived in the chamber, the stallion had raised his head at sight of him, and for a short time fire had gleamed in his large eyes. Then he had lowered his head again, and Steve had walked up to him, placing a hand upon his horse for the first time.

Now as he talked to Flame, he continued stroking the lowered head. The stallion attempted to raise his head once, but let it fall again. Steve noticed that his teeth were no longer bared, but neither was there any spirit in his eyes; nothing but tired, hopeless defeat was in them.

Suddenly Steve turned and ran up the side of the pit, crying, "Pitch! Pitch!"

In his desperation he ran solidly into Pitch, who was standing at the top. "The crane," Steve shouted. "Come on!"

Pitch followed Steve and eagerly they both grasped the crane's handle. The wheel turned beneath their combined strength, the teeth clicking rapidly as the chain wound about the wheel. Slowly, inch by inch, to the clicking of the wheel and the clattering of the moving chain, Flame's hindquarters emerged from the clutching sand and water.

"A little more, Pitch!" Steve half shouted. "Just another foot and we'll have him clear!"

Furiously they pulled at the handle until Flame was completely free of the quicksand. There he hung, the noose about his hindquarters, both of his forefeet resting upon the rim of the pit. He began struggling again, driving his forefeet into the ground, but finally stopped as though he had used up every bit of energy.

"Now what, Steve?" Pitch asked with concern.

"The rope," Steve returned quickly, his words clipped. He knew what he was going to do. "I've got to get this rope too about his hindquarters." Hastily he began uncoiling the rope he had carried with him.

"Then?"

"Then," Steve went on hurriedly, "I'm going to pull his hindquarters over as you let the chain down again. But you've got to do it slowly, Pitch."

Pitch looked puzzled. "You mean turn the wheel backward, letting him down again?"

"You don't have to turn it. His weight at the end will take care of that. You've just got to see that the wheel moves backward only a few inches at a time. You can do it by keeping hold of this bar of metal that fits into the teeth of the wheel."

"I don't see how you're going to . . ."

"You won't be letting him down into the pit again, Pitch," Steve interrupted. "You'll just be giving me more chain, so I can pull his hindquarters closer to the rim of the pit as you let down."

Pitch's face lit up. "I see now," he said. "His forefeet will act as the pivot while you swing his hindquarters over."

Nodding, Steve widened the noose he had made with his rope; then he went down to the rim of the pit, with Pitch close beside him.

Pitch's arm encircled the boy's waist as Steve hurled the lasso at the stallion's hindquarters. It took

173

several attempts before the noose settled over the quarters and encircled the stallion's girth. With Steve carrying the end of the rope, the two made their way up to the top of the pit again.

"You'd better move over closer to him," Pitch said.

Steve nodded and walked around the pit. "Let the chain down slowly, Pitch," he cautioned, ". . . very slowly."

Steve shortened the rope until it was taut, then, bracing a foot on a rock, pulled the stallion's hindquarters as far toward him and the rim of the pit as possible. "Now, Pitch," he yelled.

There was a sharp click as the wheel turned backward a few inches, then held again. Steve pulled on the rope, drawing Flame's hindquarters closer to the rim. Again there was the click of the wheel's teeth . . . and again Flame's hindquarters swung closer to the rim. Again and again the clicks sounded until the stallion's hind legs were almost above solid ground.

Flame had raised his head. He knew something was happening. Snorting, he resumed pounding his forefeet.

Pulling on the rope, Steve saw Flame's hind feet touch the rim of the pit.

"Now, Pitch!" he yelled.

And the clicks came faster as Pitch lowered away until the noose hung loosely about the stallion's girth.

For a moment Flame stood there as though his

hindquarters were no longer a part of him and had no feeling. And in that moment Steve moved forward, unheeding Pitch's sharp yell. Quickly Steve withdrew the two nooses from about the stallion; then he fell backwards as the stallion moved. From the ground, Steve saw Flame plunge heavily up the side of the pit, his body heaving and his hindquarters dragging. Then, snorting, he ran slowly from the chamber.

Getting to his feet, Steve quickly followed, but before he had reached the outer cavern he felt Pitch's hand on his arm.

"Steve!" Pitch shouted. "Let him go! You promised!"

For a moment Steve's eyes blazed and he pulled away from Pitch. "But he's hurt, Pitch. You can see that. He still needs help!"

"He can take care of himself, Steve," Pitch replied harshly. "He doesn't need you any longer. You promised me, Steve! You gave me your word . . ."

"*That I'd let him go where he pleases,*" Steve finished bitterly, "*without chasing him.*" Then, after a long pause, he said, "Maybe you're right and he can take care of himself now. Maybe he doesn't need me any longer. . . ."

Yet Steve still could hear the sound of Flame's hoofs on stone as the stallion continued running up through the tunnel, and he wondered.

14

A Boy and His Horse

THEY stood before the sea exit, the great chamber behind them. Once again Pitch looked at the hole in the outer wall, his keen interest evident in his eyes.

Steve stood a few feet away, his gaze not on the exit but directed at his feet, imbedded in the fine, white sand of the cavern's floor. He could think only of Flame.

You'd better forget him, he told himself. Forget about running after him, at any rate. You gave Pitch your word. It was a bargain you made with him. You've got to stick to it. Pitch has done his part. You've got to do yours now. Flame is free.

Steve looked up at Pitch, who was talking about the exit again. He had forgotten Flame; or at least, it was apparent to Steve, Pitch no longer cared to think about the stallion. This hole in the rock and the canal were of much more interest to him.

And he wants you to think that way, too, Steve thought. He wants you to forget Flame. Instead, think about the sea exit and the tunnels and the Conquistadores! Think about all of them, but don't think about Flame! Why did Pitch believe he could so easily forget his horse, Steve wondered. Or was he underestimating Pitch? Perhaps Pitch knew that he could never forget Flame for all the sea exits, tunnels, and lost worlds ever left by the Conquistadores!

Flame is safe now, Steve went on saying to himself. That's what you wanted, wasn't it? Pitch kept his word and helped you; now you have to keep yours. Flame is free to go where he pleases. That's what Pitch had said: *You've got to let him go where he pleases.*

Steve shuffled his feet through the sand. Yes, when he'd made that promise to Pitch he had thought that maybe the red stallion would come to him . . . that he wouldn't have to chase him any longer. He'd figured that Flame would know he was trying to help him . . . that he was his friend. And several times, when he had been close to him, Steve thought Flame really did understand what he was trying to do. But Flame was gone now, and there was nothing he could do about it. He had promised Pitch not to chase him, and he couldn't go back on his word.

"I'm puzzled by one thing, Steve," Pitch was

saying. "From all we've seen, this hole was definitely the Conquistadores' main entrance and exit. But if that's so, how did they get their armies, especially their horses, through this hole? It's wide enough . . . it must be about eight feet wide . . . but there's only about four feet of head space there. They couldn't have brought their horses through here."

Pitch went closer to the exit, peering at the dark-green moss clinging to the wall above the hole. "I wonder . . ." he began, then stopped, leaning forward to run his hand through the moss.

Steve saw Pitch's fingers probe into the heavy growth on the wall, then they bent until they were clawing, digging. And Pitch didn't stop until he had a large area cleared of the growth.

"It's wood underneath!" Pitch shouted. "Wood, Steve, right above the hole!" His hands worked furiously now, clearing away more of the moss.

The import of Pitch's discovery didn't register with Steve until Pitch had cleared an area four feet high and as many feet wide above and to the side of the hole; then Steve saw the paneled rectangular door and the beamed grooves above and below. It was a sliding panel!

Now Pitch was digging far over on the side of the hole, and finally his frantic fingers found the indentations in the wood by means of which the Conquistadores must have pulled the panel across the grooved supporting beams. Pitch thrust his fingers in the holes and tugged hard. The door didn't budge. Pitch then called to Steve, who got hold of the lower holes and pulled too. Together they forced the panel through the green moss. Then the door moved easily in the grooves, and before them was the opening to the sea, heightened by all of four feet!

Even Pitch was quiet as they looked out upon the ocean. "It's high enough now for anything," he said finally. "Even to have got their horses through." Then his gaze turned to the other side of the canal and he added, "There's a panel over there, too. They come together over the middle of the canal." His eyes gleamed. "We could get the launch through here, Steve! We could load her up with everything we find! Steve, do you realize what this means? Here we have an entrance to this lost world from the sea! We must be on the northwest tip of the is-land . . . don't you think so, Steve? We could easily find it from the boat, couldn't we?"

But Steve wasn't listening to Pitch. He hadn't listened since Pitch had mentioned that the exit was large enough "even to have got their horses through." But he wasn't thinking of the horses of the Conquistadores. He was thinking of Flame. And as he looked at the hole, now more than eight feet high, he thought how easy it would be to get a small barge in to take his horse from the island. His horse! Flame!

You shouldn't even think of it, he told himself. It's impossible.

But I don't think *anything* is impossible now, he thought soberly. And the hole is large enough to get a barge through. Even Pitch would agree to that.

But you shouldn't be thinking of it, he told himself again. You don't even have Flame. You're not going to have him. You gave Pitch your word you wouldn't chase him any longer. And there's something else even more important. What about the Piebald? What about the band? You want Flame to go back to his band, don't you? What about all your talk of this perfect breed of horse . . . of the foals now in Blue Valley and those to come? Would you forget all that just to have Flame? Was it only talk to show Pitch how much you knew about horses . . . about breeding? Was that all it was, just talk, or were you sincere?

I was sincere, he thought. I *am* sincere. It wasn't just talk. I want nothing more than for Flame to lead his band again, for he's their rightful leader. The band will never be the same if the Piebald remains their king. So I shouldn't even be thinking of taking Flame away.

Steve's eyes were focused upon Pitch, who was closing the panel door.

"I don't want to take any chances of this entrance being seen by anyone on the outside," Pitch said. "We can always open it again when we're ready to come in this way. What we've got to do now, Steve," he added quickly and with great concern, "is to go back to the dory the way we came. That's what we've got to do next."

"Sure, Pitch," Steve said. "Sure."

With Pitch doing all the talking, they walked back through the tunnel until they came to the chasm. Steve kept looking ahead, hoping he might catch a glimpse of Flame.

"We don't have to get excited about this," Pitch was saying in a high, broken voice. "We've got plenty of time to use that entrance and to do a good job of exploring this island. All I want to do now is to make sure we can get back to the dory all right; then we'll have two ways of getting to Blue Valley." Pitch stopped, and then he said frankly, "I guess I might as well admit it, Steve. I've never been so excited about anything in my whole life!"

"I know," Steve said.

Pitch looked at him as though he were seeing Steve for the first time in a long while. "But you don't seem very enthusiastic about what we've found, Steve. You're certain you realize . . ."

"What this means? What we're doing?" Steve finished for him. "Yes, I know, Pitch."

Pitch said slowly, "Then it's still the horse, Steve. Isn't it?"

Steve shrugged his shoulders. "It's still the horse, Pitch. I feel the same way about him as you do about all these other things. I just can't forget him as you'd like me to do, Pitch."

Pitch said seriously, "I know how you feel, Steve, but I'm thinking of your safety. I must hold you to your promise that you'll have nothing more to do with that wild stallion. He's savage and would kill you if you ever got close to him. You know that as well as I do. If you'd only admit it, it would be much easier for both of us."

Steve didn't want to argue with Pitch again. He felt, from what he'd seen of Flame, that the horse would not hurt him. So he said only, "I promised you that I wouldn't run after him any more, Pitch. I'll keep my word."

"And if you don't run after him, you'll have nothing more to do with him," Pitch muttered as they went along; then, changing the subject, "It's getting dark. Good thing we're going to camp out here. I wouldn't like to think of going back through the marsh at night."

They had reached the end of the chasm, with the smaller valley spread out before them, when they saw the red stallion again.

He stood knee-deep in lush grass. And the dusk cloaked his torn body in a soft veil of gray, concealing the ravaged flesh.

His long neck was stretched down to the stream and the blood-matted mane fell about his head as he drank deeply.

Pitch and Steve had stopped in their tracks. For different reasons, neither dared to move as they

182

watched the red stallion. Pitch was afraid to move, lest the stallion attacked them; while Steve was afraid his horse would run away again once he became aware of their presence.

"What'll we do, Steve?" Pitch asked anxiously. "We can't camp here with him around. He might kill us."

Steve didn't answer; his eyes were upon Flame.

Pitch said, "We can go back to the cavern. We can stay there tonight."

"We need our packs," Steve said simply. "We need food and water. We've got to stay here, Pitch. He won't bother us. I'm sure he won't bother us."

"Maybe he'll move away, farther from our packs," Pitch said hopefully. "Then we can get them and run for it."

The red stallion raised his head, ears pricked forward. Without moving his body, he turned his eyes in their direction. For all of a minute he stood there, quietly watching them; then he went back to his grazing.

"You see, Pitch!" Steve's words came fast. "He'd never bother us. He's seen us, but it hasn't made any difference to him. He's not even leaving!"

Pitch was talking now, but Steve didn't listen. He hadn't lost his horse after all! Flame was here, less than a hundred yards from where they stood! And most important, oh! most important of all, was that he hadn't run away again at sight of them. It was as

183

though the stallion had accepted them. It was almost as though he knew they had helped him. Steve felt it had to be this way.

"Steve! What's the matter with you? You're not even listening to me!" Pitch saw the specks of light in Steve's eyes, and he knew that look, knew what it meant.

Steve walked forward.

"Steve! You promised me you wouldn't go near him! You gave me your word! Steve!"

The boy's footsteps came to a halt, but he didn't turn to Pitch as he said, "I'm only going for the packs, Pitch. I'm not chasing him. I promised you I wouldn't chase him."

"But, Steve, he might . . ."

The boy was walking forward again, toward the packs, toward the stallion! Pitch stood still, not knowing what to do, but his eyes never left the boy.

Steve was talking now, calling to his horse. He had nearly reached the packs when the stallion stopped his grazing again and turned his small, wedge-shaped head toward the boy. No fire burned in the large, glazed eyes and only his blown-out nostrils disclosed any of his former hatred for the human who continued to track him. But after a short time his nostrils stilled and he went back to his grazing.

He knows me, Steve thought excitedly. He knows that I don't mean him any harm, and that's half the battle. If I could only follow through now by staying with him while he's so tired. If only I hadn't given my word to Pitch!

Steve's eyes left the stallion and rested on the packs. In his own would be the first-aid kit. He could cleanse Flame's wounds and prevent any possible infection. He wanted to take care of him so much!

But you promised Pitch, he reminded himself again. You told him you wouldn't run after Flame; that you wouldn't go to him.

But what if Flame comes to me? he thought. What if I stand still and call him and he comes? I won't be breaking my word then.

You're being silly, he told himself. He wouldn't come to you, even now after all you've done for him.

Why wouldn't he? Steve's other self argued. He hasn't run away, has he? He's standing there, not even moving, while I walk over closer to him. He knows I mean no harm. He knows I've helped him. He would have moved away by now if he didn't.

Steve turned to look at Pitch when he had reached the packs. His friend was still standing in the same spot as though he had frozen in his tracks.

If only he had come with me, Steve thought, I could have asked him. I don't want to turn back now. I want to stay here, close by my horse.

And all the time Steve continued talking, calling to the red stallion. Even though he thought of Pitch, wondering whether his friend had moved closer or not, he talked to his horse. And it seemed to him the stallion listened, for Flame paused more often in his grazing to turn to him.

Steve could hear Pitch calling, but he didn't take his eyes off Flame. If Pitch would only come over, he could reason with him, ask him to release him from his promise. If ever there was a time to win the confidence of Flame, this was it! The horse was too tired, too beaten to move away. Flame would respond willingly to all the kindness he could offer him, Steve was certain.

But Pitch stayed and Steve could only remain still, talking to the stallion, hoping he would come to him.

After a long while the red stallion, still chewing the grass, moved in Steve's direction.

Excitedly Steve watched him, yet his voice remained low.

"I've got to have patience," he said aloud to himself, knowing it did not matter what Flame heard. "I'm sure he's coming, but it'll take time. I'm keeping my promise to Pitch. I'm not chasing Flame. I went for the packs because Pitch wanted them. I don't have to go back right away. I didn't tell him I would. Hey, Flame. It's me, Steve. You're coming to me. I knew you would. I'm waiting, Flame. I've got lots of time. I'm going to stay here until you come all the way. Only a little more now. I can help you, Flame. You're sick now, but it won't be long before you're well again."

Now the red stallion was but twenty yards away

from Steve, and the boy could see the bulging veins that stood out on the sides of his head. The ears were cocked, coming almost to a point at the tips. He held long blades of grass in his mouth without chewing them. He was listening to Steve, associating this voice with the one he'd heard so often during the past few hours. His large eyes became curious as he saw the figure lower itself close to the ground, so low that he had to look down to see him.

Steve was squatting on the ground, knowing that the stallion would be less frightened of him if he made himself as small as possible. He was certain Flame was coming to him. It was just a matter of a few minutes before he would be able to touch him. He began talking once more, his hand outstretched.

Five yards away the stallion stopped to graze again. Steve moved a few feet toward him, then came to a halt, thinking it best that the stallion come all the way to him. Flame moved closer, his teeth still chopping the grass. Steve waited, his heart pounding, and he tried to keep the excitement from his voice. The stallion didn't look up again, but his head moved alongside Steve's hand. Slowly, ever so slowly, the boy moved his hand to the stallion's muzzle. Gently he touched the mole-soft skin, and there was no objection, no movement from Flame at his touch.

Tears came to Steve's eyes as he stroked the horse. "You're mine, Flame," he said. "You came to me, just as I'd hoped you would. It's the way it should be."

After a while, Steve examined the blood-clotted wounds. There was only one that caused him concern. It lay low on the stallion's thigh and the open flesh was covered with the sand and dirt of the pit. It needed to be cleansed or it would become infected. The other wounds on the stallion's strong body had already begun to heal.

Steve rose to his knees, running his hand across the blood-soaked mane. He wanted to take care of the thigh wound, but he would have to wait until the stallion had complete confidence in him.

So for a long time Steve stood beside his horse, moving with him as he grazed and always talking to him.

The valley was steeped in darkness when he heard Pitch call to him. Turning slightly, he saw Pitch only a few yards away from the packs.

"I'm all right," Steve said, his eyes turning back to the stallion. "He knows me. He came to me, Pitch. I didn't chase him this time. I kept my word."

And the voice that came out of the darkness was low and resigned. "I saw him," Pitch said. "I know, Steve. *Now* I know."

Pitch said nothing more, and when Steve turned to him again, he saw that Pitch had opened the packs and that the stove was already on the ground.

Flame moved, but Steve walked beside him, always stroking, always talking.

"Tomorrow," he said, "you'll let me help you more. Tonight we'll just get used to each other."

And when the small stove cast its light into the blackness, Pitch could see the outline of a boy and a giant horse standing close together.

15

Pitch Makes His Move

L YING on his back, Pitch stared at the stars. The moon had risen above the valley's walls, so he knew that he had slept for a little while. He rolled over on his side to take another look at Steve's blanket, knowing in advance that he wouldn't find Steve asleep in it. Pitch wondered if the boy were going to use it at all.

There was a nickering, a sudden start from the stallion, and Pitch's gaze swept in his direction. He stood silhouetted against the walls in the moonlight. Steve was beside him, and across the still night air Pitch could hear the boy's soft murmurings as he talked to the red stallion.

Would Steve stay with his horse all through the night? Would he never sleep? Pitch's own eyes were heavy and his body weary from the exhaustion of the day's work and excitement; yet his mind was too active and Pitch tried his best to quiet it.

You don't have to worry about Steve any longer, he told himself. You're silly if you do. The stallion won't harm him. You've seen that for yourself. This relationship between Steve and the stallion is something you don't understand, but you saw for yourself that the stallion came to Steve. He always will be his horse from now on. Maybe he always has been, for all you know. Maybe Steve has always known this red stallion, just as he says. Maybe it *is* his Flame. Who are you to doubt it? Not after all you've seen today. You've read of such things happening between man and horse, although Tom once said it never actually happened. *It's story-book stuff* . . . those were his exact words. Tom with his big hands. Tom with his bull whip and bottle. Tom, who thought there was only one way to conquer a wild horse. *You've got to break him with your own hands,* he would say. *You've got to show him who's boss!*

I wonder what Tom would say to all this, Pitch thought. I wonder if he'd believe it even if he witnessed it, as I'm doing.

But Tom never would have Steve's patience. Never would he have waited for this stallion to come to him, urging him on only by kindness and by his voice.

191

Pitch listened to the sound of Steve's voice and thought again: It's Steve's voice that's winning the confidence of this stallion as much as anything. I'm sure Tom couldn't talk that way even if he wanted to. I don't think there *are* many people in the world who could talk that way to a horse. A voice like that has to come from the heart. It's like a mother talking to her child . . . that's the only comparison I know.

But stop thinking about it, Pitch told himself almost angrily. Maybe Steve can do without sleep, but you can't. You're getting old, my boy. You need your sleep. Steve's young. He's all right . . . he'll always be all right. You don't have to worry about anything. And if you have to think, you'd better think about the sea exit and what you might find in some of those other caves in Blue Valley. Better still, don't think of anything until tomorrow. Tomorrow you can start looking for the way back to the dory, too. Steve will want to stay with his horse. You might as well accept that now, because nothing is more important to Steve than what he's doing now. He might not like you to go alone, but just tell him you want to look around the caves all by yourself. Tell him you can get around faster that way, since you know exactly what you're looking for. That's a laugh, your getting around faster without Steve. . . .

Pitch's eyes left the boy and horse and turned to the stars overhead again. After many minutes, heavy

Pitch could hear Steve's soft murmurings
as he talked to the red stallion

lids dropped over his eyes and his breathing became deeper as he fell asleep.

When Pitch opened his eyes again, the gray light of dawn had cleansed the sky of stars. For a moment Pitch could have been anywhere; then he heard the shrill call of the stallion and it pierced his sleep-laden mind, shattering it back to reality. Quickly he turned to the blanket beside him. It was empty but wrinkled, and at least he knew that Steve had lain down on it sometime during the night.

As he glanced over toward the walls, he noticed that already the stove was burning.

A hundred yards beyond, Pitch saw the stallion slowly moving away from Steve, who stood watching him. Steve was holding a pot in his hand; he turned just then and started back toward the stove.

Pitch rose to his feet and went over to the stove. He waited until Steve was within earshot before asking, "Have you been up the whole night?"

There were dark circles under Steve's eyes. "I slept a little," he said, placing the pot down on the ground.

"What have you been up to?"

"He's got a bad cut on his left thigh," Steve replied. "It was dirty. I cleaned it just now."

Pitch cast a quick glance at the first-aid kit that lay on the ground beside Steve's pack. The package of gauze was open.

"I just used hot water and soap," Steve was saying as he bent over the kit. "I want to put some iodine on the cut a little later on."

"But maybe iodine is too strong for him, Steve," Pitch protested. "It'll burn like the devil. Have you thought of that? It might undo all the good you've done."

"I thought of diluting it with water," Steve answered, his voice troubled too.

"Did you have much of a job getting the cut cleansed?"

"A little," was all Steve said.

Pitch knew it had been more difficult than Steve would admit. It was one thing to stroke the stallion and another to cleanse his lacerated flesh. "Let's have some breakfast," he finally said with attempted lightness. "I'm sure hungry."

While Pitch boiled the water, Steve opened a can of ham and prepared the powdered eggs. They spoke little while breakfast was being cooked, and it was only when they were eating that Pitch said, "I suppose you want to stay here with him." He didn't wait for Steve's reply, but went on. "I thought I'd go back to Blue Valley. There are some caves I'd like to look into. Wouldn't be surprised at what I might find in them."

"But we were going to . . ." Steve paused, then continued in a steady voice, ". . . we were going to look for the way back to the dory."

"That can wait a while," Pitch returned. "Or I might even stumble on it." He smiled as he saw the concern on Steve's face. "And don't think for a moment that I'll get lost again. I guess we've both learned our lesson on that score. I'm not taking any chances, Steve, so don't you worry about me. I still have the chalk, and I'll be able to mark every inch of the way if I happen to go into any of those tunnels. No more arrows like the last time. And I'll have burning torches this time . . . they don't break." He laughed before adding, "But I probably won't even look for the way back, Steve. As I said, there's plenty of stuff in those caves near the waterfall to keep me busy."

"But Pitch . . ."

"You'd only slow me down, Steve," Pitch interrupted. "I can save time by looking alone. And after all, you're more interested in Flame than in anything I might find. You have your work, Steve . . . I have mine. Let it go at that."

Steve studied Pitch for several minutes before saying, "I'll be back at the cliff tonight, Pitch." Then he dropped his eyes to the food in front of him as he said, almost inaudibly, "Thanks, Pitch."

They had finished breakfast and were washing the pots when Pitch spoke again. "I'll wait until you put the iodine on him. You might need some help."

Steve turned and looked at his horse, who was now

grazing some distance away. "I wonder," he began, then stopped, going to the first-aid kit.

He poured some of the iodine into a pot and added water. "You think that's enough, Pitch?"

"I think so, Steve. You've cut it about half. It shouldn't be too strong for him now. He'll feel it, though. You're still sure you'd better not just leave the wound alone?"

"I can't, Pitch," Steve returned solemnly. "Infection could so easily set in now."

Pitch didn't reply, and they sat watching the stallion in silence.

The gray light of early morning had given way to the brightness of day when Steve rose to his feet. He went to the first-aid kit and, taking up the package of gauze, tore a long piece from the roll, which he folded carefully; then he went over to the stove and picked up the pot containing the iodine solution.

It had been difficult enough cleansing the thigh wound only with water, for he had had to stand quietly beside the stallion for many hours, stroking him until he could draw the cloth across the cut. It would be much more difficult now, because although the iodine was diluted it would still smart and burn when applied to Flame's open wound. And Steve knew that as a result his horse might forever be afraid of him.

Pitch asked, "Are you going now?"

Steve didn't answer, but the steps he took away from the stove were all the reply Pitch needed. He watched Steve walk down to the floor of the valley. He heard him call to the stallion who was grazing fifty or more yards away from him. Flame raised his head, and although he returned to his grazing, seemingly ignoring the boy, his searching muzzle and chopping teeth brought him closer and closer to Steve.

Steve made no attempt to hide the cloth or pot. As he approached the stallion Flame looked up at him and at the pot the boy was holding. Blowing out his nostrils, Flame turned away from Steve. But he didn't run, and Steve followed, talking all the while.

When Flame reached the stream and stopped to drink, Steve placed the pot down on the ground and dipped the gauze in the antiseptic until it was thoroughly soaked; then, taking the dripping cloth with him, he approached the stallion.

Steve stroked the horse as he drank, then dipped his left hand in the stream and wet Flame's matted mane. His hand didn't stop when it came to the end of the mane, but traveled across the muscled withers until it rested upon Flame's haunch. Just below Steve's hand was the open wound.

Steve held the cloth in his other hand. He hesitated a moment before taking this next step, knowing full well that possibly it might be the last time he would be able to stand so close to his horse; for he had

198

decided to hold the cloth on the wound as long as he could. He would not dab as he had done that morning, when he had been using only water.

Flame stomped his hind foot and swished his long tail about. He had stopped drinking and was moving to a new spot to graze. Steve walked along with him, his hand still upon him.

Finally the stallion came to a halt again. Steve glanced at the folded gauze in his hand, then at the flesh ravaged by the Piebald. Now was the time. The muscles in his face became taut, and then his hand moved forward, slowly at first until the gauze was but a few inches from the wound. He kept talking to the stallion as he placed the cloth over the wound and pressed it firmly onto the flesh.

For a fraction of a second the stallion stood still; then, as the diluted iodine penetrated his raw skin, he snorted and sidestepped quickly.

Steve watched him go, knowing the job had been done.

Flame galloped in long, fast strides until he reached the walls; then he slowed down to a trot before he finally stopped. He turned to the boy, shrilling loudly, as though in reproach; then he went back to his grazing.

It stung him only for a few seconds, Steve thought. He really didn't act up as much as I thought he might. And it's done now.

Hearing footsteps behind him, Steve turned.

"You got it on him?" Pitch asked.

Steve nodded, and together they walked back to their packs.

A short time later Steve watched Pitch cross the valley floor and disappear within the gorge; then the boy sat down upon his unrolled blanket.

Flame was grazing about a quarter of a mile away.

Steve's eyes rested on the stallion for a long time; then he thought, I'd better leave him alone for a little while longer. If I don't go after him, perhaps he'll come to me. I don't want to push him. I want him to come to me. It's better that way.

Large, billowy clouds appeared overhead, but through them burst the morning sun, warming the upper valley with its light. Steve, welcoming the sun's rays, lay back on the blanket, his head turned to one side and his eyes resting on Flame. The stallion had moved from the shadows along the walls out into the sun, and his body glowed a fiery red. His long tail no longer trailed the ground but swished constantly about his body.

"Flies," muttered Steve. "They're starting to bother him."

The boy's eyes closed. He was tired. He'd rest for a while, then go to his horse again. It had been a long night, and as he'd told Pitch, he hadn't had much sleep. But it had been worth it. Now he'd just rest for a little while. He wouldn't go to sleep, just rest.

Resting was as good as sleeping, anyway. But he didn't want to rest very long, either. There was so much to do today. No more iodine, just being with his horse. He wanted to be around him a lot so that before long Flame would take his presence very much for granted. Flame would never know why he had cleansed his wound and put the iodine on it. He'd remember only that it had stung him and he hadn't liked it. But it had had to be done. There was plenty of time to make amends . . . plenty of time.

Steve's eyes remained closed as the sun's warmth slowly relaxed his taut muscles. He felt his face becoming hot, and for a moment he didn't even think of Flame. And in that moment he fell asleep.

He didn't know how long he had lain there when suddenly he felt something soft and wet against his face. Opening his eyes, he saw Flame standing close beside him!

The stallion's muzzle moved about the grass, and Steve realized that was what had touched his face a few minutes before. He lay there quietly, but his eyes devoured the stallion.

Don't rush to him, he told himself. Take it nice and easy. Take him for granted, too. Just pretend you've always been with him. You can sit up now, but don't rush to him yet. Take it easy as you did last night. He likes you or he wouldn't be here. He's getting used to you, Steve!

Slowly Steve rose to a sitting position, talking to

his horse, his eyes going to the thigh wound. It was still clean, but he'd have to watch it for any infection that might develop. Shifting his gaze to the other cuts on the stallion's body, he found that already hard scabs had formed over them. There was no sign of pus, no infection in any of them.

Flame's head rose a few inches from the ground, his neck extended. He shook his mane and his body twitched.

Steve saw the large flies hovering above him and about his girth. Flame's tail whipped at them like a lash; then he sniffed the ground and moved away until he had found a slight depression in the ground. Carefully, he lowered himself down to it and rolled over on his back. Long legs thrashed the air as he grunted in pleasure. Finally he turned over on his side again before rolling over once more and driving his back into the soft earth.

Steve waited until the horse had risen to his feet and had shaken himself before going to him. Anxiously he looked at the thigh wound and to his relief found it to be still clean, for it was too low on the thigh to have touched the ground when the stallion rolled over.

Gently Steve's hand swept over the giant body until it came to rest upon the mane; then he stroked the slender neck and small head which had jerked up at his touch.

Flame's flashing eyes turned from side to side, but he remained still; then, as though satisfied there was nothing to fear, he went back to his grazing.

Hour after hour Steve stayed with his horse, talking to him as though Flame understood everything he had to say. He walked with him about the valley while the sun moved slowly across the sky and began its descent. And, very often, as he looked at the glistening body beside him, studying the strong limbs and well-muscled withers, chest and shoulders, all of which indicated tremendous strength, and the sculptured head and neck that indicated a perfect breed, he thought of what it would be like to ride this horse. But he never let himself think of it too long or too often, for it was enough, at this moment, that he walked beside him. Yet he could dream . . . and dream he did as he watched the red stallion throughout the day. He saw himself riding Flame about the valley and, at times, could even feel the surge of the stallion's giant muscles beneath his knees.

But with the setting of the sun behind the walls to the west, Steve left his horse.

I'll leave everything here, he thought; I'll be back in the morning. I'll just take my blanket . . . Pitch will have enough food for both of us.

Steve went over to Flame, stood with him a few minutes more, then, reluctantly, turned toward the gorge that would take him back to Blue Valley. He hadn't walked very far when he heard Flame's shrill whistle and, turning, saw the stallion moving slowly toward him.

Steve stood still while the horse stopped to graze again. The boy's eyes took in the ever lengthening shadows, and he knew he had to go now if he was to get back to Pitch before dark. So, turning, he walked on. Behind him he could hear Flame's hoofs as the stallion followed him.

Steve didn't stop until he had reached the ascent to the gorge; then he turned and found Flame close behind him. Going up to him, he stroked the pink-skinned muzzle.

"I'll be back, Flame," he said. "I'll be back tomorrow."

The red stallion whinnied and thrust his nose into the hollow of Steve's hand. There was no hatred or menace in his large eyes now; nothing was there but wonder. When Steve turned away from him, going up to the entrance to the gorge, the stallion did not follow; instead he turned in the direction of the valley floor as though he wanted none of the trail ahead.

"Tomorrow, tomorrow," Steve repeated aloud, as the walls closed in upon him. "And the day after . . . and the one after that. Oh, if only I could be with him always!"

Always!

16

Winged Hoofs

T OMORROW . . . *and the day after . . . and the one after that.*

Five days came and went, with each morning's sun finding Steve in the smaller valley. He lived for the hours of daylight when he could be with his horse. Yet he reckoned the passing of time only by the condition of the scabs upon Flame's wounds, scabs which hardened until finally they began cracking off, giving way, piece by piece, to the new skin beneath.

And each night back in Blue Valley, Pitch listened as Steve spoke of the stallion's speedy recovery and of Flame coming to him at his call. After the first few nights, Pitch had let himself think that Steve's enthusiasm for the red stallion would lessen, but again he found he still did not understand the relationship between the boy and the horse; for if anything, Steve became more intense, his voice more excited, as he told Pitch about Flame during the nights that followed.

And Pitch, when Steve had finished talking each evening, would tell the boy of *his* day's explorations, would show him the sextant he'd found, the pistol with the handle etched in gold, small ammunition and the dagger. But he knew that Steve never really looked at them, and thought only of his horse. Even when Pitch told Steve how well he was learning his way around the tunnels and that one day soon he was certain he would come upon the way back to the dory, he wondered if the boy actually listened to him. It was as though Steve didn't care about ever leaving this valley . . . as though he wanted to remain here always with his horse.

It was only when Pitch spoke of the Piebald, which he did more often now, that Steve's eyes disclosed his attentiveness. The Piebald worried Pitch. The Piebald stood between him and his complete freedom of the valley, for Pitch feared the black-and-white stallion more with every day that passed.

"If it weren't for him," he told Steve one night, "I could get around this valley a lot easier. I'm certain I could find plenty by doing some digging down there, but he keeps me away. Oh, I'm not thinking of right now, Steve, because I have plenty of stuff to take back on this trip. I don't want to bring back too much, you know, for fear someone will get wise to what we've found. But later on I'd like to look around the valley floor . . . do a thorough job of it, I mean. I can't with that Piebald around." And then Pitch had stopped, his gaze unwavering as he looked at Steve. "But I could do it if Flame led the band again," he went on. "When do you think he'll be coming back, Steve? He's going to return to his band, isn't he? He won't just stay in the smaller valley, will he?"

Steve had merely shrugged his shoulders, and before Pitch could continue, the boy had changed the subject.

This dawn, as Steve walked through the gorge toward the smaller valley, he thought: Should it be this morning? Have I waited long enough? Flame lets me put my weight on him. He's never given me any trouble. What difference will it make to him whether I'm leaning on him or sitting upon his back? I just want to sit there, that's all I want to do.

For the first few days, Steve had only dreamed of riding his horse, but then dreams had given way to a great desire actually to press his knees close to the muscled withers, to sit astride his horse. So for many hours he had stood and walked patiently beside Flame, his weight resting more and more heavily upon the red stallion.

The smaller valley opened before Steve, and the

boy's eyes eagerly sought Flame. He found him in the center of the valley. Already Flame had turned in his direction with ears pricked forward, alert to the slightest sound, and head craned high.

Steve called to him, but even before the words had left his mouth, the valley echoed to the shrill whistle of the stallion; then Flame was moving toward him, no longer hesitant as in earlier days, no longer stopping to graze, but taking long, swift strides, his long tail and mane whipping the air like searing flame. He swept across the valley floor until he reached the ascent to the gorge, where suddenly he came to a stop. Shaking his head, he whinnied repeatedly, his eyes never leaving the boy.

And as Steve walked forward to meet him, the brightness left the boy's eyes for a fraction of a second, to be replaced by soberness.

Never has Flame come to me while I have been near the gorge, he thought. Why? Is it because . . . Steve paused in his thinking, his face troubled. No, it isn't that, he thought. It hasn't anything to do with it. I won't think that way.

Then he had reached the stallion and there was room only for affection in his eyes. He burrowed his hands in the fiery mane as he talked to his horse.

After several minutes, Flame lowered his head to the grass and Steve slid his hand over the sleek back. For a while he studied the wounds, all of them nearly healed except for the one on the stallion's thigh. But there was no sign of infection under the heavy scab and in just a few days it too would be well healed.

Moving to one side of Flame, Steve raised both hands to the stallion's back. The boy stood there quietly for a few moments before leaning more heavily upon the horse. Finally most of his weight rested upon the stallion.

"Steady, Flame," Steve heard himself say.

Flame raised his head, turning to the boy before going back to his grazing once more.

Steve's hands moved over the stallion's back again; his fingers were nervous and uncertain now that the moment was near. Flame stomped the ground with his hind leg to rid himself of flies.

I can't very well get on his back, Steve thought. He's much too high for me. But I could mount him from that rock over there. He'd follow me over there.

The stallion's small ears pricked forward as Steve moved slowly over to the rock. Without hesitation, the horse followed the boy.

The rock was three feet high and flat on top. Steve stood up on it. It was as good as anything he could want as a springboard from which to mount Flame. He was aware of that, and yet still he hesitated, his right hand upon the red mane.

Finally he raised his other hand to the stallion's back. Half his weight now rested upon Flame. There was a moment when Flame turned to him, his eyes wide with wonder. Steve talked to him, and the stallion went back to his grazing again.

He's got complete confidence in you, Steve told himself. He knows you wouldn't hurt him. Lean more upon him; then move over onto his back. Don't jump, though. The slower and easier you do it the better.

Steve knew there was no turning back now. He was going to ride his horse!

Gradually the bulk of his weight fell upon Flame until only the balls of his feet were resting on the rock.

One swing will do it now, he told himself. One easy swing. Keep hold of the mane in case he bolts. Remember, you don't have any bridle or saddle. You've got only your voice. Keep talking to him every second. You have to . . .

But he had already swung one leg from the rock and it was closely followed by the other as, with his hands resting upon Flame, he bore down on the stallion with all his weight.

Flame's head came up quickly, but for a fraction of a second he didn't move. And just then Steve pressed his knees against him and wrapped his fingers in the long mane. All the while he continued talking to his horse.

He felt Flame's muscles grow taut beneath his knees. He talked faster, desperately trying to keep his voice from wavering. Flame crabstepped, forgetting his grazing. Then the tautness left his muscles and suddenly he bolted.

Steve, his face close to Flame's neck, could use only his voice in an effort to slow the ever lengthening, ever faster strides of the stallion. But all he heard himself saying was, "Flame! Flame!" The wind tore the words from his mouth.

For some time the stallion ran with his ears flat against his head, yet there was no plunging to his gait, no attempt to unseat his rider.

Leaning forward, Steve pressed his mouth close to the stallion. "It's me!" he cried. "Flame! Flame!" Repeatedly he shouted the horse's name into the whipping wind.

The stallion's ears pitched forward, and between them Steve could see the stream cutting across the valley. When Flame came to it he swerved sharply, and Steve moved his body with him. For the first time he felt a part of his horse!

It had come to him with the suddenness of the stallion's shifting gait as he had turned across the valley. Now there was nothing fearful about the ever lengthening strides or the wind that tore at his tearfilled eyes. Leaning forward, Steve moved with his horse, glorying in the surge of powerful muscles beneath his legs. No longer did he feel that the stallion was separate from him, that he was riding Flame. It was entirely different now. It was as though he and the horse were one. He was Flame! He thought the same, felt the same! They were running because they loved to run, because this was the way it was meant to be!

As they turned from the stream, heading down the valley once more, Steve heard himself clucking to his horse. Clucking to the rhythmic beat of thunderous hoofs upon soft turf and thinking that all this was far beyond his wildest dreams. For this wasn't riding but being a part of a giant stallion who was his horse, his very own! It was flying without wings! It was wonderfully effortless and easy. He belonged there on Flame's back.

He let the stallion run, his tight fingers about the mane long since relaxed, as was his body. He continued clucking softly, his head close to the sleek neck. And beneath his knees he felt the restrained power within Flame and knew the stallion was running at only a fraction of his utmost speed.

Flame galloped with his ears pricked forward; occasionally one or both cocked back as Steve called to him. Finally he slowed to a long, easy lope.

They had approached the ascent to the gorge when Flame swerved quickly away from it, snorting at the same time; then he turned toward the center of the valley, slowing to a canter until he was crabstepping on prancing hoofs.

When Flame came to a stop, Steve sat still for a moment, while the stallion stretched his long neck down to graze. Then Steve slid off, but his hands still

Leaning forward, Steve moved with his horse

rested upon Flame. He knew that now he could never part with his horse.

Nothing mattered now but Flame. Steve faced everything now. There was no sense in kidding himself any longer, he felt. He had been reluctant to talk to Pitch about Flame's return to his band because he knew full well that Flame *wasn't* going back! He had known it for many days . . . ever since the stallion had first turned away from the gorge leading to Blue Valley. Flame didn't want to go back. The Piebald had left his mark not only on Flame's flesh, but deep in his very heart. And it was Flame's fear of the Piebald, together with his loneliness, that had made it easier for Steve to win the stallion's love.

Knowing all this, Steve had looked upon the Piebald with new eyes, aware of the viciousness, the reptilian cunning of the new leader. And he realized full well that if Flame had even the slightest tremor of fear within his body, he would be killed if he met the Piebald in battle.

But he won't have to fight him now, Steve thought, as he stood beside his horse. I won't have him killed. He means more to me than anything else. I don't care about the band. Let the Piebald lead them. Let it be the end of this breed, as long as I have Flame. I'll take him away. I'll take him home. . . .

17

Steve's Decision

<hr>

THAT evening, as blue shadows blanketed the valley floor below, Pitch listened to Steve tell of his desire to take Flame away from the island. His face grave, Pitch said nothing until the boy had finished.

After a moment of silence, he said slowly, choosing his words with great care, "You haven't thought this out, Steve. You don't realize the consequences of what you're planning to do. Even if you are successful in getting Flame off the island, what will you do with him . . . a wild stallion? And there's Tom. What do you think his reaction will be? What of all this?" With his arm Pitch gestured toward the towering walls whose summits seemed to reach the darkening sky. "It could possibly be the end of this lost world, you know . . . a world only the two of us know." Then he looked straight at

Steve, his words clipped and his eyes unwavering as he asked, almost angrily, "And what about your band, Steve? What about all your talk of maintaining this perfect breed of horse? It wasn't long ago that you said you'd do *anything* to keep the band as it is. *You* were going to find some way to *kill* the Piebald. Remember?"

Steve's tanned face flushed as he turned from Pitch's accusing gaze to look at the dark figures of the horses as they moved quietly in the dusk.

"I didn't mean to be unkind," Pitch said quickly. "I'm sorry, Steve. It's just that I'm finding it difficult to keep pace with your reasoning. Why are you so certain that Flame won't return to his band? Is there actually a reason or is it your riding him that has brought about this sudden decision to take him away?"

Pitch waited for Steve's reply, but it was several moments before the boy said in a very low voice, "He's afraid."

Pitch leaned forward. "I didn't hear you, Steve."

Steve turned to his friend. The words came hard, but he repeated them. "He's afraid . . ."

"Afraid? Afraid of what?"

"Of . . . of the Piebald." Steve's voice wavered, for Flame's fear of the black-and-white stallion was something he had wanted to keep to himself. But there was no alternative now; he had to tell Pitch everything. "He's not coming back, Pitch. He'll never return to his band while the Piebald is there. He won't go near the gorge leading back to Blue Valley. I've known it for a long time."

Pitch remained silent, but his gaze swept to the band and to the Piebald in the valley below.

"I can't leave him alone, Pitch." Steve's words came faster now. "What good would come of it? He'd stay in the smaller valley until he died . . . and he's not meant to be an outcast like that. He needs affection. He's my horse, and I want him."

"So much that you don't care what happens to the band," Pitch said, without turning to the boy.

"That's unfair, Pitch," Steve said angrily. "I can't do anything about them. There's nothing you or I can do about the Piebald."

"No, I guess there isn't," Pitch admitted. "But there are other things to be considered, Steve. What of Tom's reaction to such a horse as Flame coming from this island? What do you think he'll do?"

Steve's eyes met Pitch's as he said defiantly, "He can't take him from me. He said I could have any horse I wanted if I stayed here two weeks. You heard him, Pitch."

"Yes, I know," Pitch replied. "And he won't go back on his word; I know him well enough for that." He paused before adding, "But I wasn't thinking of his taking Flame away from you, Steve. I was wondering what he'd do about this island, once he's seen Flame. What he and others would do, I mean."

"I'll tell him I found Flame on the reef," Steve returned grudgingly. "I won't tell him any more than that."

"I don't think he'll believe you," Pitch said gravely.

"Even if he doesn't, he'll never find his way into Blue Valley," Steve returned with a confidence he didn't entirely feel.

"Perhaps not, Steve. Still . . ." Pitch paused and his gaze left the boy as he added, "You see, I'm being selfish, too. You want your horse, and I want everything I can possibly find that was left behind by the Conquistadores. Naturally I'd like to keep this world to ourselves."

"But I would, too, Pitch," Steve said quickly. "We'll just have to take a chance that no one else will find it." He stopped, then asked slowly, "Have you thought of what Tom's reaction will be to the things *you're* bringing back . . . the pistol, the spurs and all that other stuff? What will you tell him when he asks where you found them, Pitch?"

The man dropped his eyes as he admitted, "I'll tell him I found them on the reef."

"But I don't think he'll believe *you*, either," Steve said slowly.

218

They were silent for a long while as dusk slowly
gave way to night and stars needled their way
through the ever-darkening sky to hang like a
jeweled crown above the valley. It was a wondrous
view that lay before them, this world of beauty and
intrigue that had been untouched for hundreds of
years. Now it was theirs alone. But each asked
himself: For how long will it be only ours?

Finally Pitch said, "I still think you should leave
Flame here, Steve. What will you do with him, if you
get him to Antago?"

"I'll take him home with me," Steve said slowly.

"It'll cost money. More than you have."

"I'll cable my father when we go back to Antago
for the barge," Steve said, but his voice was hesitant,
unsure.

"How do you think he and your mother are going
to take it . . . your asking for money to bring home
a horse?"

"It'll be all right. I'm sure it will. Dad will
understand," Steve replied quickly.

But will it be all right? Steve wondered. *Would
they send him the money? Would they understand?*

"I have to take him home," Steve told Pitch. "I
couldn't leave him on Antago . . . with Tom."

"No," Pitch agreed. "You couldn't do that and
still keep your horse." Rising to his feet, he added,
"Then maybe you'd better not think too much about

taking Flame off this island before you learn what your folks have to say. Maybe we'd better let it go at that for the time being."

"I'm sure they'll understand. I have some money saved. It shouldn't cost too much." Steve paused, then asked, "Can we look for the way back to the dory tonight, Pitch?"

Nodding, Pitch turned to him. "Yes, we can do that, Steve. I can show you a tunnel that might be it . . . at least, it seems to be going in the right direction."

"And we'll keep looking every evening until we find it, won't we, Pitch? I'll leave Flame a few hours early each day, so I'll have more time to look for it with you. Is that all right, Pitch?" Steve asked anxiously.

"Yes, Steve," Pitch replied. "That's all right."

Three nights went by, with Steve following Pitch through the tunnels for many hours, marveling at his friend's newly-acquired knowledge of this underground world. Pitch walked quickly in the light from his burning torch, stopping only to point out chambers he had found in previous days. Always upon the walls Steve would see his friend's chalked lines; and when they came to intersections there would be figures and letters of which only Pitch knew the meaning. But when Pitch came upon tunnels he had not been through before, his pace would slacken, and after a few minutes it would be he who decided whether or not they should continue onward.

Confidently Steve placed himself in Pitch's hands, knowing there were few tunnels left through which Pitch had not already walked and that one night soon they would find their way back. Each night, too, even as he followed doggedly at Pitch's heels, he would think of what it would be like to have Flame at home, where he could be with him always. And in his mind he framed the cable he planned to send to his father, for his father would understand while his mother might not. He would wire, *"Please cable me . . ."*

How much money will I need to ship Flame home? he wondered. I'll have to find out before I send my cable. If it's only one hundred dollars I have that much saved up. In that case, I'll say, *"Please send me my one hundred dollars. Urgent. I have found my stallion."*

No. Perhaps *stallion* isn't the best word to use. It might frighten them. I'd better make it *horse.* I'll say, *"Please send me my one hundred dollars. Urgent. I have found my horse."*

It still doesn't sound right, he thought. They'll never understand how important it is to me from that. I'm sure it would be much better if I put it in a letter. I could really tell them how I feel about Flame in a letter. I'll write to Dad. He should understand.

He knows how I feel about horses better than Mom does.

It was early the fourth evening when their burning torch disclosed the fork in the tunnel ahead. Steve saw Pitch come to an abrupt stop, then move close to the right wall.

And in the light each saw it . . . a large arrow, drawn by them days, or was it years, ago? Simultaneously they both cried out, but then afterward they stood quietly before it, neither saying a word.

For both knew they could go now, any time they pleased. And they could return to Blue Valley just as easily. Also, they could open the upper doors of the sea exit and carry away what they both wanted so desperately. But what would be the outcome? Would it mean that this world would be theirs no longer? Would Tom and others search for the entrance to Blue Valley until they found it?

As they linked arms they smiled, each wondering what the other was thinking.

18

Last Day

STEVE sat quietly on Flame's back, his hands softly stroking the sleek neck. He had been astride his horse since his arrival in the valley at dawn. Throughout the day he had sat there, longer than ever before. For this day was different from any of the others . . . this was his fourteenth day on the island, and tomorrow morning he and Pitch were returning to Antago.

"But I'll be back in a few days," he told Flame. "I'll be back to get you, and then we'll never be separated again."

We'll never be separated again.

Would it be like that, he asked himself over and over again. Would his mother and father understand his love for Flame as he thought they would? Would Tom keep his word to let him have any horse on Azul Island once he set eyes on Flame? And if he did, would Tom believe him when he told him that he had found Flame on the reef?

Steve's eyes left his horse for the western walls that separated them from the sea. No, he thought, he won't believe me . . . that much I know. How could he possibly? He'll know we've found something, and he'll look for it himself. But he won't find the way. He'll never find the right tunnel or the sea exit.

Steve's hands fell about the stallion's neck as he placed his face close to his horse.

Raising his head, Flame cocked his ears, moved forward a few strides, and stopped to graze once more.

Steve let him graze only a short while longer before leaning forward and saying, "Let's go, Flame." He clucked softly in the stallion's ear and Flame's head came up with a start; then he moved forward on dancing hoofs as Steve squeezed his legs slightly about him.

Steve buried his head in the stallion's flowing mane as Flame broke into his long, loping canter. Then the horse's strides quickened until he was in full gallop. Steve's knees pressed close to the glistening red body as he felt the surge of giant muscles. He clung like a burr to the stallion's back while Flame swept about the edge of the valley floor, and always Steve's soft clucking was an accompaniment to the beat of pounding hoofs.

Flame circled the valley many times; then Steve ceased his clucking and called upon the stallion to stop. Flame responded slowly, his strides gradually growing shorter until he was in his loping canter. When he came to a halt, Steve slid off. Already the sun was sinking behind the western wall. It was time to go back to Pitch.

He turned to Flame, pressing his head close to the soft muzzle.

"I won't be around tomorrow," he whispered, "nor the next day . . . or the few that follow. But I won't be long, Flame, and when I do come back it'll be to take you away with me. Then we'll be together always."

Steve stayed with his horse for a while longer before leaving him. As he walked up the slope leading to the gorge, he heard the sound of Flame's hoofs following him. When he turned around, after he had gone some distance, Flame was close behind.

Steve went to his horse again, his face troubled. This, he knew, was the nearest Flame had ever been to the gorge leading back to Blue Valley. Did it mean that Flame wasn't as afraid of the Piebald as he believed? Would Flame one day go back to Blue Valley?

Steve stood close beside his horse, rubbing his hand across the silken coat. When he turned away again he heard the sound of Flame's hoofs behind him once more. He was almost at the gorge when the hoofbeats stopped. Turning around, Steve saw his horse standing still, watching him with large, curious eyes. The stallion shook his fiery head and whinnied.

Steve called to him, but Flame remained still. After a while he went back to his grazing and Steve left the valley.

All through the gorge and across the marsh, Steve thought over and over again: Will he return to his band after all? Was I wrong in thinking he'd live alone, an outcast, rather than go back and face the Piebald? But he's not going to live alone. I want him. I'm going to take him away. I don't want him to fight the Piebald!

As the boy reached the top of the hollow leading from the marsh, he looked ahead at the black-and-white stallion. The Piebald was grazing with his band in the center of Blue Valley. Steve watched him for several moments before ducking below the tall cane and moving up the valley.

And always, as he walked along, the Piebald was there before him, as vivid as though Steve were actually looking at him. He saw the close-set eyes, one blue, the other white. He saw the hatred, the viciousness gleaming in them. The long mulelike ears were pulled back flat against the heavy head as the stallion bared his teeth and shook his massive body.

Then, in his mind, Steve saw the Piebald go forward to meet Flame, as he had done that first day. Heavily he ran, the earth shaking beneath his thunderous hoofs. And during the next few moments, Steve relived every blow of pounding hoofs on flesh, every second of raking, tearing teeth during the terrible fight.

He came to an abrupt stop, the palms of his hands wet and a feverish light in his eyes. "Stop thinking of the Piebald!" he said aloud. "Flame isn't coming back. There will be no fight. I'll have him away from here soon. I'll have him for my own."

But when Steve walked forward again, he asked himself: But what if he does come back? What if he fights the Piebald while you're away? What if he's killed? Flame is smarter and faster, but if he's just a little afraid he'll be killed by the Piebald. The Piebald is no blundering bruiser, but crafty and cunning, and he knows how to use his weight to his advantage.

"I've got to get Flame away soon," Steve muttered. "I won't have him killed *now*."

Steve's pace increased until he was running, his body crouched low and hidden from the Piebald by the tall cane.

Ahead, high on the cliff, Pitch would be waiting, and very early tomorrow morning they'd start for Antago. Every moment, every day counted now, if he was to save his horse from what he felt would be certain death beneath the hoofs of the Piebald.

The following morning it was still dark when they finished their breakfast. Steve packed hurriedly, then turned to find Pitch looking out upon the valley, his pack untouched. The gray of dawn began to appear in the sky to the east. Below, the band was already grazing.

"Let's hurry, Pitch," Steve said impatiently.

But it was another moment before Pitch gave his attention to his pack. "Have you ever seen anything like it, Steve?" he asked. "Where else on earth could anyone find the magnificent beauty, the solitude and peace we have here?"

Steve didn't reply, for he was watching the Piebald move from his band to the pool directly below. And when he again turned to Pitch, he found that his friend still hadn't packed; he was gazing at the pistol, the sextant, the spurs and the few other things he had found, which were all neatly placed in a small pile beside his pack.

"I'd better put them in first, hadn't I?" Pitch asked. "I want to pack them in the bottom, so no one will see them. I may have to leave some of my equipment behind, unless you have room for it in your pack."

"I can take a little," Steve replied quickly. "I've some room."

Pitch looked out at the valley again.

Steve said once more, "Let's go, Pitch. It'll be light in a few minutes." He bent down to pick up Pitch's equipment, but momentarily his gaze too swept down the valley. Yes, he thought, soon it will be light, and it will be the first morning I haven't been with Flame since I found him. I wonder if he'll miss me. I wonder what he'll do. But the sooner I get Pitch out of here, the sooner I'll be back.

Pitch bent down beside him, but he only handled one of the spurs, without placing it in his pack. "Steve," he said slowly, "do you think we're doing the right thing?"

Steve looked at him questioningly.

"I mean . . ." Pitch began, then he paused. "Maybe I should leave all this here. Wouldn't it be better not to take chances on having anyone learn about Blue Valley? It's rather wonderful having a world all our own, Steve. I . . . I guess I've changed in the past few days. What I mean to say is I'd rather leave everything here just as we found it . . . and then come back to it," he added, his gaze dropping. "No one will ever know about Blue Valley that way and we can come back to it every summer . . . when you're able to be here, I mean. We won't arouse anyone's curiosity. We'll just be camping, Steve. No one will ever know what we've found."

Steve had listened in silence, knowing what it meant for Pitch to give up his treasures for something he valued even more. When Pitch had finished, Steve found that he couldn't meet his friend's eyes, and he asked himself: Would you give up Flame to keep this world for yourself . . . for yourself and Pitch? And he thought selfishly, no, I couldn't do that. For much as I love this valley, I love Flame even more. And if I want him to be safe, I must take him away from here . . . away from the Piebald.

"What do you think, Steve?" Pitch was asking again. "Should I leave everything here? Do you think it best, too?"

"No, Pitch," Steve replied slowly, "I think you'd better take it with you." He paused. "I'm going to take Flame away from here, you know. And when Tom sees him . . ." Steve left the sentence unfinished. When he looked up, Pitch's eyes were upon him. And he realized from what he saw in them that Pitch doubted he would be able to take Flame away, doubted his parents would ever send him the money to get Flame home. But he doesn't know them, Steve thought. He doesn't really know them.

The boy stood up and walked over to his pack, while Pitch stayed behind, still fondling the heavy iron spur.

After a while Steve heard Pitch say, "I'm going to leave them behind, Steve. I've decided for myself. I've made up my mind." And when the boy turned to him, he saw that Pitch's eyes were bright and that his face had lost the tautness of the past few days. Steve suddenly felt very old and very tired.

Pitch began packing his equipment, paying no further attention to his newly acquired possessions until he had finished. Then he said, "I want to hide them, Steve. I'll only be a few minutes."

Steve nodded, and Pitch picked up his treasures one by one. When he started for the cave behind them, Steve looked anxiously at the eastern sky. The gray had given way to the golden light of the sun.

I'm always with Flame by this time, he thought. I'd be standing close to him, maybe even riding him by now. I know he's looking for me, wondering where I am. He'll miss me. I'm sure he'll miss me. But it won't be long before I'll be back, and he'll wait for me. I'm sure he will.

Pitch came out of the cave just as the sun appeared above the eastern walls and the valley gleamed brightly as the grass, heavy with dew, picked up the sun's rays. The band was grazing a short distance from the pool, with only the young, spindle-legged foals running about, slipping as they turned too sharply on their uncertain legs. The Piebald grazed alone with only an occasional glance at his band. Confident and defiant, he stood there with nothing to fear.

"The sun's up," Steve said as Pitch reached for his pack.

Pitch fell in behind Steve as they made their way up the trail. "It makes little difference to us in the tunnels," he remarked.

"But we want to get back to Antago before dark," Steve replied.

"We'll make it with hours to spare," Pitch returned.

They had reached the black hole from which the stream poured when Pitch called out to Steve to stop for a moment. "One last look, Steve," he said.

"But Pitch . . ." Steve began impatiently. "We'll be coming back in a few days."

"I know, Steve. But just in case we don't. Just in case . . ." Pitch left the sentence unfinished, but Steve knew what he meant.

Together they watched the water plummet down to the pool below; then Pitch looked about at Blue Valley, but Steve turned his eyes toward the marsh, where just beyond, he knew, Flame was waiting for him. The vapors rising from the hollow were becoming heavier with the heat of the sun's first rays.

"Soon I'll be back, Flame," Steve muttered. "Very soon. Wait for me."

"What'd you say, Steve?" Pitch asked.

"Nothing, Pitch. We'd better get going."

"Yes, I guess we should. All right, Steve."

But the boy, his eyes still fixed on the hollow, didn't move.

"I'm ready," Pitch said. "I said I'm ready, Steve," he repeated. He was about to give the boy a light push when he noticed Steve's blood-drained face and wide, staring eyes. Glancing quickly at the hollow, he too saw the weird, ghostly sight before them.

The stallion stood just below the top of the hollow, his giant body enshrouded by clinging, smokelike mist; then he moved forward a few strides, and the vapor gave way to the bright sun that turned his red coat into living, breathing fire.

Flame had returned to Blue Valley!

19

Raging Demons!

———

OR many minutes the red stallion stood there. His head was raised high but he made no move or sound.

Trembling, Steve awaited his shrill clarion call of challenge but none came, and silence prevailed throughout the valley. Steve turned quickly to the Piebald, who still grazed, unmindful of the red stallion's presence, for he was upwind.

Steve's gaze swept back to Flame. More minutes passed, yet Flame made no move toward the Piebald. But Steve could see his head begin to turn back and forth as though he were looking for something.

Pitch said, "He's after you, Steve. He's not after the Piebald."

Yes! Steve thought. Yes, that's it! He's looking for *me!*

The boy's heart beat faster, and the blood surged through him, flooding his pale face. Quickly he turned, making his way back down the trail, and it wasn't until he had reached their old camp site that he felt Pitch's hand upon his arm. Angrily he pulled away; Pitch's grip loosened, then tightened again and held. Furiously Steve turned upon him, the white heat of anger making his words indistinct.

"You young stupid fool, Steve!" Pitch shouted. "Where do you think you're going? You'll be killed if you go down there! The Piebald . . . there'll be a fight!"

Steve twisted his arm free of Pitch's grip and ran headlong down the trail. Halfway to the valley floor, he flung his pack off his back without stopping. Behind him, Pitch followed crying, "Steve! You fool! You fool!"

Blindly, the boy turned from the trail as he reached the floor of the canyon, and ran across the grass. He didn't head for the cane, but ran swiftly across the floor in a straight line, heading directly for his horse.

A short distance away from him, mares squealed in fright as they saw him running past; foals kept close to their mothers; and a few hundred yards away from them, the Piebald jerked his head up, snorted and plunged forward, his ears pinned back, his eyes wild and frightening.

Unmindful of his danger, Steve still ran forward. He saw nothing but the route ahead that would take him to Flame, heard nothing but the sound of his own running feet.

Then Pitch's scream shattered the boy's frenzied mind and stilled his heart. Turning, he saw Pitch close behind him, but Pitch was standing still, frozen in his tracks, his face turned away. And it was then that Steve heard for the first time the thunderous hoofs that shook the very ground beneath him. His face was drained of all color as he saw the Piebald coming at them. Wildly, Steve ran to Pitch. "The pool!" he shouted. "It's our only chance!" And before the words had left his mouth, he had Pitch by the arm and was pulling him toward the water.

They took one step for every stride of the Piebald. The pool was twenty-five yards away, and twice that distance behind them was the plunging black-and-white stallion, snorting now as he neared them.

Pitch's running steps faltered and his breath came heavily. Steve ran beside him, his head half turned to the onrushing stallion. He saw the bared teeth, the beady eyes, and knew the savage brute meant to run them down.

Ten yards more to the pool, only a second more, but it was too late, for the Piebald was upon them! Steve shoved Pitch toward the pool and flung himself to the side. The stallion turned with him, his shoulder striking the boy's arm and twirling him around. As Steve hit the ground, he saw Pitch dive headlong into the pool. The Piebald slid on his haunches as he tried to stop. Frantically, Steve climbed to his feet, but even before he was fully up he was taking the fast, pounding steps of a sprinter just off his mark. He was five yards from the pool when the Piebald turned upon him again. But Steve flew over the ground and plunged into the water.

When he came to the surface, he heard Flame's wild clarion call. High-pitched, shrill, and piercing, it claimed the valley as its own. And when it died away, the valley echoed to the repeated neighs of the mares as they rapidly formed their tight circle, with hindquarters facing outward and foals secure in the center of the ring.

Through the cane rushed the giant red stallion, the tall stalks bending and breaking beneath his weight. Without stopping, he entered the arena, running up the valley floor until he was within a few hundred yards of the Piebald, who had turned to meet him. Flame stopped only long enough to cry his shattering challenge again, then came onward, carrying the fight to the Piebald.

The black-and-white stallion plunged forward, his eyes livid with hate as the tall, long-limbed red stallion galloped to meet him and the valley resounded to their pounding hoofs of death.

Steve and Pitch had pulled themselves up to the bank of the pool. They said nothing, their eyes upon the stallions. Steve's shirt was torn where the Piebald had struck him, and his arm hung limp at his side, but he felt no pain.

Any second now the bodies of the two horses would clash, for Flame was moving in faster and faster. It frightened Steve, for he well remembered the red stallion's caution in the first fight, when he had let the Piebald carry the fight to him, avoiding the heavily plunging black-and-white stallion with the skill and agility of a trained fighter.

But he's not afraid, Steve told himself. He's not afraid! And then he said aloud, "Pitch, he's got to win. He's just got to!"

Pitch muttered, "You did it. He wouldn't have come on if he hadn't seen . . ."

But Pitch's words were lost in the heavy, terrible clashing of bodies as the two stallions met with such fury as could only be kindled by two wild, savage animals whose only intent is to kill.

They had met head on, neither seeking to avoid the other, and each consumed with an unearthly hatred that turned them into raging beasts horrible to see.

Seemingly unmindful of the Piebald's superior weight, Flame rose with the black-and-white stallion after the first resounding clash that had locked them together. His teeth tore at the neck of the Piebald, seeking a hold which once secured would never be released. Screaming in rage, the Piebald drove his heavy hoofs into Flame's shoulders, and the red stallion reeled back from the force of the blows. Plunging forward, the Piebald sought to drive Flame to the ground. But the red stallion twirled and in an instant had raised his long hindquarters, his hoofs battering his opponent's face. Staggering, the Piebald took the blow and rose to meet Flame as the red stallion circled and moved in on him again. They were locked together once more, raking teeth their only weapons, and the screams of both reached a new and terrible pitch.

Each lunged for the other's neck. But always there would be a twisting, a turning of bodies that avoided death by fractions of inches. More and more the Piebald sought to use his brute weight by throwing himself repeatedly on the red stallion. But he was fearful of Flame's teeth, that moved with the speed of a striking snake.

"Why doesn't Flame keep away from him? Why doesn't he?" Steve babbled.

"He knows what he's doing," Pitch said quickly.

But as the fighting at close quarters continued with neither giving way, the Piebald's superior weight began to tell on Flame. His movements were slower and several times the Piebald's raking teeth had almost secured their hold on Flame's neck before the red stallion was able to twist away.

The Piebald fought with renewed energy as he hurled his thick body again and again at his opponent. Crazed eyes of blue and white were wild, now that the moment of triumph was near.

Forelegs wrapped about each other's neck, they screamed and bit and tore at ravaged flesh, their snapping teeth like rapiers in the hands of expert swordsmen—striking, parrying, never ending.

Demons rather than horses, their bodies wet with sweat and blood, they stood on hind legs for many minutes, savaging each other mercilessly. Then slowly, ever so slowly, it was the red stallion who gave ground. Screaming and following up his advantage, the Piebald hurled his massive body more heavily upon Flame until the red stallion, squealing in pain, wrenched himself clear of the Piebald.

In the few seconds that he twirled away, Steve thought it was over and that Flame's only chance for his life was to run . . . to run as he had done before. And Steve heard himself screaming to his horse. "Run! Run!"

The red stallion pivoted around the Piebald as the black-and-white stallion plunged at him and missed. Again Flame had the opportunity to flee, and for a second he stood still, breathing heavily.

"Go, Flame! Go!" Steve shouted at the top of his voice. But his words fell away beneath the sound of the wrenching and cracking of bodies as Flame rose to meet the Piebald's return rush.

Nevertheless, Flame's tactics had changed, and it was as though pain and the last few agonizing minutes when he had tasted defeat had given rise to intelligence over frenzied fury. Now he moved in quickly, striking hard, but never staying long before moving away again on lightning hoofs. He was patient, waiting until he was ready before going forward with bared teeth and battering forefeet. And

239

when the Piebald charged, Flame avoided him on winged feet, moving with swiftness and agility. Sometimes he would turn, and his hind legs would catch the Piebald with tremendous power. For many minutes Flame whirled, circled, reared, pummeling with slashing hoofs, tearing with raking, ripping teeth. And always he would leap clear again before the Piebald could hold him close.

Finally the Piebald, too, changed his tactics. No longer did he rely upon weight alone. No longer did he charge ruthlessly, blindly, to be cut to ribbons by his agile opponent. He too awaited openings, all the while maneuvering his burly body into a position where he could fight the red stallion once more at close quarters, where his weight would give him an advantage. His small eyes gleamed red as persistently but cautiously he forced the fight, rearing high to catch and hold his elusive enemy.

The hoofs of both thrashed the air, sometimes finding their mark and striking solidly upon hard flesh. Snorting, squealing, each waited for the opening that would mean destruction for the other.

Flanks heaved and their breathing became heavier, but still the furious tempo of the fight went on. Now, more than ever before, each was wary of the other. This fight had lasted too long. Both were tired, each knew his chance would come soon.

Furiously the Piebald charged. Flame moved away a fraction of a second too late, and he felt the weight of the Piebald upon his shoulders. He swerved, trying to get clear, then stumbled and fell to the ground. Frantically he regained his feet, turning to face the Piebald, who reared high to crush him. Flame rose to meet him. As their bodies met, the Piebald strove to lock the red stallion close to him. But this time Flame did not attempt to leap clear again; instead, he drove his battering forefeet hard into the Piebald, staying close and forcing the fight.

The Piebald tried to recover his balance, but the red stallion continued pounding and his teeth sank into the thick neck, secured their hold, *and held!* Screaming in pain, the black-and-white stallion went down, and only when he was flat on the ground did Flame release his death grip; then he rose above his

opponent and came down, driving his pounding forefeet into the still form that lay beneath him.

When it was over, he raised his wet, blood-soaked head, and the valley was filled with his shattering call of triumph; then he turned to his band.

Their faces white, Steve and Pitch rose uncertainly to their feet. And it was only Pitch who found words to describe his emotions. "Horrible . . . horrible," he said shakingly.

Steve stood there, his glazed eyes unseeing. Then, slowly, life came back to his numbed body and he thought, it's over . . . over, over. And never do I want to see another fight like it.

For several minutes they stood in silence, their eyes following the red stallion as he circled his band.

He's alive, Steve thought. He's killed the Piebald.

And then Pitch's hand was upon his arm, pulling aside the torn shirt, probing, but Steve felt nothing.

Pitch said quickly, "It's broken. I've got to get you out of here." His arm went around the boy's waist. "You're up to it, aren't you, Steve? It'll be hard, but we've got to get you to a doctor."

Listlessly, Steve nodded and walked beside Pitch to the trail. They had gone only a short way when Steve stopped and said, "But Flame's hurt, Pitch. He needs care."

"You do, too," Pitch said patiently. "He can take care of himself. He always has."

"Yes," Steve repeated slowly, "he always has."

The mares had broken their ring and foals ran excitedly about, neighing to their mothers. Arrogantly Flame watched them as he trotted about with them. It was only when Steve and Pitch neared the trail that he turned to them. His small head was craned high as he whistled to Steve; then he came toward him in his long, loping canter. He stopped a few yards away and Steve went to him.

Pitch stayed behind, watching as Steve flung his arm about the ravaged neck. Then he saw the boy's gaze move critically over the torn flesh until once more he pressed his head close to Flame's soft muzzle.

They stayed that way for several minutes before Steve stepped back and the red stallion whirled and ran back to his band.

When Steve returned to Pitch, he said only, "They're clean. He'll be all right, I guess."

They walked up the rocky trail until they had reached the tunnel; then they both turned back to look at the band. Flame was trotting about, his long mane and tail flowing. Once he came to a stop, and gazed upward at the ledge upon which Steve stood. His whistle filled the valley before he turned away, his eyes once more on his band.

Steve realized then that his horse belonged there; that never, never could he take him away now.

Without a word or another backward glance, he followed Pitch into the tunnel.

20

Their Lost World

———

THEY left the quiet of the doctor's office for the noise and busy traffic of Chestertown, Antago.

As they stood upon the stone steps, Pitch said softly, "It's like being awakened from a long dream, Steve." His gaze left the crowded street, where automobiles and people were mixed in a crazy tangle, and fixed itself on the splint and sling around the boy's arm.

Pitch's gaze was so intent that Steve asked, "What's the matter, Pitch?"

The man's eyes never left the sling as he said, "If it wasn't for your arm, I'd probably think it had all been a dream."

Their eyes met and Steve couldn't help thinking how strange Pitch had been acting since their arrival on Antago a few hours ago. "But you know it wasn't a dream, Pitch," he said. "We know everything is back there, just the way it was. We can go there again whenever we like, just as you said. No one will ever know what we've found. No one."

Pitch looked down at his feet for a while, then glanced at the busy street again. "It's so different now," he said. "I'd forgotten how . . . I mean, it's just . . ." He paused, groping for words.

"I know, Pitch," Steve said helpfully. "But it makes what we found all the more precious. We have a world of our own, Pitch! Just think of it. A world of our own!" He stopped then, his eyes afire with the full realization that he and Pitch actually possessed a lost world which now, in the clamor of Antago's busy traffic, seemed beyond belief.

But Pitch never turned to him, nor did he say a word. He just stood there, his eyes darting uneasily about the street.

Steve watched him in growing bewilderment. "Pitch," he finally said with effort, "what's the matter with you? You're not the same guy . . ."

"You mean," Pitch interrupted, "I'm not the same guy I was in the Valley. Maybe not, Steve. Maybe not." He paused and glanced again at the people in the street. "I guess they did it . . . and all this." He nodded his head in no particular direction. "We're part of it now. We have responsibilities."

"I don't get you, Pitch. What are you driving at?"

"Back in the Valley," Pitch said slowly, "I was a boy again. I was thrilled at finding our secret world. I

245

wanted nothing more than for us to keep it to ourselves. But I'm afraid we can't . . ."

"Pitch!" Steve shouted. He had his hand on his friend's arm. He whirled him around, forcing him to look his way. "You wouldn't! You can't!" His eyes were blazing in anger.

"Steve! Steve! You've got to understand the responsibility we have. We've made a discovery that should be made known to the world!"

"But, Pitch . . ."

They stood looking at one another, each trying to make the other understand.

"I feel the same way you do, Steve, about having our very own world. Please believe me, Steve," Pitch pleaded. "I meant every word I said on the island about keeping it to ourselves. But now that we're back, now that we're a part of civilization again, I can't help feeling that it's our duty, our responsibility, to make known our secret."

"And Flame?" Steve asked bitterly. "What do you think will happen to him and his band? Have you forgotten all about Tom, Pitch? You know as well as I do what he'd do with those horses. And even if I could have Flame, I wouldn't sacrifice the others to Tom. I won't let you do it, Pitch." Steve's voice was cold and determined. "I don't know just how I'll stop you, but I will."

"Stop talking that way, Steve," Pitch said angrily. "You know that I don't want the horses to fall into

Tom's hands any more than you do. All I'm asking is that you talk this over with me, realizing, as I do now, that we have a great responsibility on our shoulders. Do you think it's easy for me to give up what we've found? Don't you realize how much I'd like to continue with my explorations?"

"I'm sorry, Pitch," Steve said.

"It's just that I'm older, Steve," Pitch sought to explain, "and I do realize the importance of our discovery."

Steve looked at him, trying to understand all that Pitch was telling him; but it was difficult, in view of his love for Flame and the band.

"Pitch," he said finally, "don't you think there are many places in this world where archaeologists and historians are working all by themselves? Isn't it possible," he continued, his words coming faster now, "that there are many men like you, who have found something of real historical value, yet who will keep their work to themselves until they're ready to make public what they've found?"

"I suppose so, Steve. Yes, I'm certain there must be. I have a friend, a historian, who's been in Tibet for a number of years on a secret project." Pitch was looking at Steve now, and slowly the tiny pinpoints of light were reappearing in his eyes. "You mean . . ." He paused. "You think that I . . ."

"I think," Steve said quickly, "that here's your chance to work on something really terrific all by yourself. You can do all the explorations you've ever wanted to do. It's the opportunity of a lifetime, Pitch."

Eagerly, yet a little afraid, Steve watched Pitch's face. He still saw the doubt and uncertainty there, the lack of confidence.

"You could do it, Pitch. You really could," Steve said.

"Do you really think so, Steve? I'm pretty much of a greenhorn. But I've read a lot. I know a great deal about the Conquistadores. Still, it's such a big job . . ."

"No greenhorn could have done what you did in those tunnels," Steve said sincerely.

Pitch was trying hard to stem the flood of eagerness that he could feel surging through him. But he failed utterly, and it was there in his eyes, shining brightly for Steve to see.

Pitch's words came fast now. "I'm sure I could do a good job of it, Steve. Really, I am. I could map every one of those tunnels. There must be many more than we found. And chambers as well. I could . . . Oh, Steve, there are so many things I could do. Perhaps even a book. Yes, I'd write a book about it eventually. Why, it might even make me famous!" He stopped, blushing and becoming embarrassed. "I mean that some historical society might find some good use for it." Then he paused again, his face a little troubled. "But it will take a long time to do the right kind of a job, Steve. It may take me years, doing it all alone."

Steve smiled. "That's what I figured, Pitch. Exactly what I figured."

"But I'll do a thorough, competent job of it," Pitch said with determination.

Steve took Pitch by the arm as they made their way down the stone walk. "I know you will, Pitch. And you won't be alone all the time, because every summer I'll be back . . . early every summer."

At the gate, Pitch turned to Steve. "I can't tell you how much better I feel. I knew that by talking it over with you we'd work something out. I never would have thought of going ahead alone and, perhaps, if I were lucky, making a name for myself. But I'm ready for it now, Steve," he said, smiling. "I'm just as confident as they come!"

They walked down the street with Pitch protecting Steve's broken arm from the crowd. They were passing a shipping office when Steve called Pitch's attention to a large blackboard. "Due next Monday," they read, "the *S. S. Horn*. Sails same day. Cargo space available for Puerto Rico, Haiti, and the United States. Mail closes seven A.M. day of departure."

"She's on schedule," Steve said.

"I'm going to miss you, Steve."

"It won't be long before I'll be back again," the boy said. "But I'll be missing you, too, Pitch."

In the next block, they found a taxi and climbed inside. Their driver was about to pull away from the curb when a large truck drew up alongside. The man behind the wheel of the truck shouted to them, and Steve was the first to recognize Tom.

Steve sat back in his seat, but Pitch leaned out the window and greeted his stepbrother.

Then Steve heard Tom say, "I've got a job to do, but I'll be out to the house right after. Didn't think you'd last the two weeks on Azul. Tell the kid I said that. Tell him he won his bet and can have any horse on the island he wants . . . if he still wants any of 'em," he added, laughing; then Tom had his truck in gear and went on ahead.

"Well, you've got your horse," Pitch said, smiling.

"Yes," Steve agreed. "I have him, all right."

And once more Steve was riding Flame, his face pressed close to the silken neck as the red stallion swept about an arena whose towering, yellow walls were the only spectators.

FLAME

SATAN

BLACK MINX

BONFIRE